JESS THE BORDER COLLIE
The Promise

As relieved as she was that the puppies had been born alive and unscathed by Orla's accident, Jenny felt a small stab of disappointment. Carrie had so badly wanted a boy puppy.

Mr Palmer picked up the last of the litter and carefully turned it over.

'And the last one is . . . yes, it's a wee boy!'

'Oh, thank goodness!' said Jenny. 'Oh, how lucky! How lovely! I can't believe it.' She threw her arms round Ellen, who hugged her back.

'That's Carrie's pup,' Jenny said. 'That's Charlie – Carrie's gorgeous little Charlie.'

The PROMISE

LUCY DANIELS

Hodder
Children's
Books

a division of Hodder Headline

Special thanks to Ingrid Hoare

Text copyright © 2000 Working Partners Ltd
Created by Working Partners Ltd, 1 Albion Place, London W6 0QT
Illustrations copyright © 2000 Sheila Ratcliffe
Jess the Border Collie is a trademark of
Working Partners Limited

First published in Great Britain in 2000
by Hodder Children's Books

A Catalogue record for this book is available from the British Library

ISBN 0 340 77849 0

Typeset by Avon Dataset Ltd, Bidford-on-Avon, Warks

Printed and bound in Great Britain by
The Guernsey Press Co. Ltd, Channel Isles

Hodder Children's Books
a division of Hodder Headline
338 Euston Road
London NW1 3BH

1

'Hello Jenny!' said Mrs Turner with a welcoming smile.

Jenny Miles felt herself relax as she steadied her bike against the whitewashed wall of the house. It was a good sign that Carrie's mum was her usual cheerful self. These days, Jenny never knew quite what to expect when visiting Cliff House, but the expression on the face of her best friend's mother was always a reliable clue. Only last week, Mrs Turner had opened the door with a blotchy, tear-stained face

– and predictably, Jenny had found that Carrie was terribly unwell.

'Hello, Mrs Turner,' she replied brightly, shrugging off the backpack she wore. 'How's Carrie feeling today?'

Jess, Jenny's Border collie, sat down on the paved path outside the door, his tail swishing vigorously from side to side.

'Chatty,' Carrie's mum replied, 'and hungry, which is good. It's so *lovely* to have her home from the hospital! Come in and say hello. And you, Jess!'

Jess responded immediately, bounding into the house in search of Carrie. He always accompanied Jenny when she went to see the Turners. Jenny could sense that Jess missed Carrie and the rambling walks the three of them shared, as much as she did. Carrie's illness – leukaemia, a type of cancer of the blood – meant that walking an energetic dog was out of the question.

'Is that you, Jen?' came a voice, and Jenny followed it into the sitting-room. Jess had run ahead and already had his front paws up on the sofa. He was trying to lick Carrie's face and she was giggling helplessly. 'Get off!' she squeaked, pushing weakly at his chest.

'Down boy!' said Jenny, laughing, too. The collie's

snowy white socks immediately dropped to the floor and he hung his head, his ears flat.

'Oh, he's lovely,' said Carrie, rubbing his ears. She was sitting on the sofa next to a table on which a large and complicated-looking jigsaw puzzle was spread out. Taking a proper look at her friend, Jenny noticed the peculiar colour of Carrie's skin. It was a bruised yellow, and the colour had spread into the whites of her eyes. Jenny tried not to stare, not wanting to make Carrie to feel in the least bit uncomfortable.

'What have you got there?' Carrie asked, pointing at the backpack.

'This?' Jenny lifted it. 'Lots of things for you. Chocolates, comics and that magazine you like . . .'

'You're spoiling her, as usual!' Mrs Turner had come into the room. She went over to push back a curtain and open a window. The summer sunshine streamed in, making the cosy little room even brighter. Carrie's mum was an artist, and her love of colour was reflected everywhere in the house. This room had a flowery wallpaper with a background the colour of honey. It made Jenny feel as if she was sitting in the middle of a sunny meadow. Up until recently, Cliff House, had always been a happy and lively place to visit.

'I deserve spoiling!' said Carrie, rummaging in the bag for the chocolates. 'Hmm . . . thanks, Jen.'

Jess's ears pricked up and he edged a bit closer. His nose twitched at the sugary smell.

Jenny laughed. 'No, Jess, they're not for you.'

'How are the two love birds?' Carrie asked mischievously, her cheek bulging with a chocolate-covered toffee. She offered one to Jenny, who shook her head.

'They're fine,' Jenny grinned. She knew that her friend was talking about her father and Ellen, his new wife. Even though Ellen had been the long-term, live-in housekeeper at Windy Hill, the sheep farm where Jenny lived with her dad, their sudden decision to marry had taken everyone by surprise.

'They're planning a visit to Canada, to see some of Ellen's family,' Jenny said. 'It'll be a kind of late honeymoon, I suppose.'

'That will be good – for both of them,' Mrs Turner put in, popping back into the room with two glasses of Coke. 'Your father could certainly do with a break.'

Jenny's father, Fraser Miles, farmed a huge herd of blackface sheep across land that had been given to him by his parents-in-law. When Jenny's mother, Sheena, had been killed in a riding accident, he had been more determined than ever not to give in to his shock and grief, but to repay her family's trust in him by turning the farm into a thriving business. He had worked hard, and it had paid off.

'What's it like, having Mrs Grace for a stepmother?' Carrie asked.

'Oh, not much different, except that I call her Ellen now. It's *almost* – but not quite – the same as having Mum around. Ellen was already part of the family, really.'

Jenny didn't want to seem disloyal to her mother. It had taken her, and her nineteen-year-old brother Matt, a period of adjustment to come to terms with the thought that Ellen Grace would be sharing her father's life permanently, but now they were both pleased.

'And guess what?' Jenny added, 'Ellen has left all the photographs of Mum around the house, just exactly where they were.'

'That's so nice,' Carrie smiled. 'Most people would have put them away somewhere. I suppose it's because they were such good friends. I think your mum would approve!'

Mrs Turner put her head round the door. 'I'm going out to do a bit of weeding in the garden,' she said. 'Shall I let Jess out? He can have a wander around.'

'Good idea,' Jenny said. She gave Jess's glossy black back a pat and then he trotted after Carrie's mum.

Carrie had swung her legs up onto the sofa and was resting her head against a cushion.

When she looked again at the peculiar, ghostly glow of her friend's skin, Jenny couldn't help being reminded of a Hallowe'en mask she'd once seen. 'How are you?' she asked hesitantly. Carrie inspected her fingers, then began to chew carefully along the edge of a nail. Jenny waited. Something inside her made her dread the answer.

'The bone marrow transplant hasn't worked,' Carrie stated bluntly. 'And now I've got a problem with my liver — which is why I've turned this horrible mustard colour.' She sounded calm and seemed resigned to the situation.

'But . . .' Jenny felt lost. 'The marrow from Sarah Taylor's bones is the same as yours. It *must* have worked.' Sitting in the chair opposite the sofa, she felt her heart begin to speed up.

'Well, it hasn't,' Carrie said and helped herself to another chocolate. She shrugged. 'Sometimes, it just doesn't work.'

'Will you go back into hospital — will they have another go?' Jenny asked in a small voice.

'There isn't any point,' Carrie explained. 'The

only thing to do now is to try and get by on my medication and the chemotherapy. But, you know, I may not. Get by, I mean.' Carrie was watching Jenny intently, as if waiting for a reaction.

'What?' Jenny said, hating the way her face felt as though it was draining itself of blood. Carrie seemed so unaffected by what she was saying, it was as if she was talking about somebody else's illness. But Jenny knew that her friend was drawing on an incredible inner strength that she had found since her recent bout of leukaemia.

'I know I can say these things to you, because you're my best friend,' Carrie said, speaking quietly and looking Jenny straight in the eye. 'I can't talk to my parents like this. I don't want to upset them.'

Jenny nodded, lost for words, suddenly engulfed by her own sadness.

'I'm not afraid to die. Not *really*,' Carrie said, sighing. 'It can't be as bad as everyone thinks.'

'Stop it!' Jenny jumped up from her chair. 'Carrie, stop! You're not going to die! You're *not*.' She wound her arms round Carrie's thin shoulders and tried to pull her into a hug.

But Carrie gently pushed her away. 'Now, you're not going to go all mushy on me, are you?' she smiled.

Jenny's felt her legs begin to wobble and she sat

down suddenly on the carpet in front of the sofa, resting her elbow on the corner of the table. 'You won't die,' she said again. How would I get by without you?' A tide of anguish and self-pity washed over her, and Jenny's eyes brimmed with hot, stinging tears.

'You've got other friends,' Carrie reasoned. 'There's Fiona, and David.'

'It's not the same,' Jenny mumbled. 'They're not *you.*' The tears were flowing freely down her cheeks now.

'And Jess,' Carrie went on. 'You've got Jess, remember.'

Into Jenny's mind came a picture of Jess, lying in a soft blue blanket in her arms just hours after his struggle to be born. He'd had a damaged leg and Jenny's father had been adamant that there was no room on a working farm for a lame dog. The furry bundle had gazed trustingly up at her with his big bright eyes, and Jenny had seen in them such fierce determination to live that her heart had gone out to him. She managed to persuade her father to change his mind and eventually he'd agreed that Jenny could keep the puppy if she looked after him herself.

'Oh, Jen, don't cry,' Carrie pleaded. 'It will upset my mum.'

Jenny hurriedly wiped her sleeve across her face and sniffed loudly.

'Look, you've got to make me a promise,' Carrie said. 'Are you listening?'

'Yes,' Jenny whispered.

'A promise you can't break? You must promise.' Carrie frowned.

Jenny could see she meant business. She looked into her friend's eyes and nodded sombrely.

Carrie continued, 'If I can't live, then you must live *for* me. OK? I mean I want you to do all the things we did together, just as if I was there with you.' She took a sip of her Coke and still Jenny said nothing. 'Make a pact with me? You'll have a go at things, and have fun? Do you promise?'

Jenny gave herself a little shake. She had been lost in a memory of a day at school when Fiona MacLay had been bullying her and Carrie Turner had come to her rescue. Fun-loving and spirited, the flame-haired new girl had surprised Jenny by choosing her as a friend.

Jenny blinked back her tears and swallowed hard. She had to be strong for Carrie. She was determined to battle the terrible sadness and fear that gripped her. She stood up. 'I promise,' she said, smiling.

'Promise what?' said Mr Turner, coming into the

room with carrier bag full of groceries.

'Girls' talk, Dad,' Carrie said dismissively.

'Hello, Jenny!' he said. 'Phew! Graston market is murder on a Saturday morning!'

'Hello, Mr Turner.' Jenny's voice was steady.

'I hear that your Jess is going to be the father of a litter of pups, Jenny,' he said, grinning

'Yes,' she replied. 'Isn't it great? And Carrie's going to have a puppy, isn't she?' Jenny felt that, somehow, becoming the owner of a puppy would mean Carrie *had* to get well. It would at least give her friend something to look forward to and to focus on.

'Yes,' Mr Turner confirmed. 'Carrie can have one of Jess's litter, if all goes well.'

'A boy,' Carrie said. 'I want a boy puppy, just like Jess.'

'Well, we'll have to wait and see,' Mr Turner said and Jenny saw his shoulders slump and a shadow cross his face. 'Right, I'll just go and put these things away in the kitchen,' he said. Then he added; 'Oh, Carrie lass, I found you that book you wanted.'

'Thanks, Dad!' Carrie said, smiling and standing up. She wobbled alarmingly and put out a hand to steady herself on the arm of the sofa. Then she repositioned the little woollen beret that she had worn ever since her wonderful, wild red hair had fallen out due to the chemotherapy, and stepped round the table. 'Come with me into the kitchen,' she said to Jenny. 'This is a great book that I've wanted for ages! It's full of—'

But Carrie never got any further. She suddenly doubled over, and then slid sideways onto the carpet, rolling onto her back as she landed.

Jenny gasped and covered her mouth with her hands. 'Carrie?' she whispered. Then, she opened her mouth and shouted as loudly as she could. 'Mr Turner! Mrs Turner! Come quickly!'

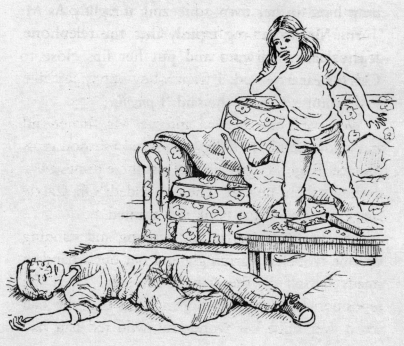

Within seconds, both Carrie's parents had rushed into the sitting room. Jenny watched helplessly, with tears already streaming down her face, as Mrs Turner fumbled to feel her daughter's pulse and Mr Turner stroked Carrie's forehead, murmuring her name repeatedly, his voice strained with shock.

'Phone the hospital, Thomas,' Mrs Turner said urgently. 'Get Doctor Wallis – and tell him it's an emergency. I'll get her medication.'

Jenny was suddenly alone in the room with Carrie. Impulsively, she knelt beside her friend and took her limp hand in her own, squeezing it tightly. As Mr Turner began talking rapidly into the telephone, Jenny leaned forward and put her lips close to Carrie's ear.

'I promise, Carrie,' she said. 'I *promise*.'

2

Early the following morning, Jenny was woken by Jess. His warm breath on her cheek startled her and she opened her eyes to see him looking down at her, a troubled expression in his gentle eyes.

Jenny found that she had fallen asleep on the big, wide sofa in the sitting-room at Windy Hill. She was still fully dressed, but someone had thrown a quilt over her, and her shoes lay neatly, side by side on the rug. Jess's pink tongue darted out, licking the back of her hand.

'Hello,' Jenny said softly and tickled his chest. Her eyes felt swollen and sore and her throat ached. She remembered curling up here beside Ellen after supper the previous evening and giving vent to her misery over Carrie. She had cried and cried, until Ellen had given her a mug of hot milk and honey that had soothed her into a dreamless sleep.

'We decided not to move you. You looked so peaceful.' Jenny turned her head to see Ellen in the doorway, and Jess's tail thumped out a welcome on the floor. 'You've woken your mistress, Jess,' Ellen scolded.

Jenny smiled and stroked the collie. Short of getting up onto the sofa, he had manoeuvred himself as close to Jenny as he could get. 'It doesn't matter,' she said. 'What time is it?'

Ellen looked at her watch. 'Just gone eight-thirty,' she said 'Your father and Matt have gone off to mend the barn roof. How are you feeling?'

'OK.' Jenny rubbed her eyes. 'But my eyes hurt.'

'I'm not surprised, love.' Ellen smiled kindly. 'I rang the Turners, after you'd gone to sleep,' she went on. 'Mr Turner said the doctor had visited Carrie and she was asleep as well.'

Jenny sat up and pushed her tangled fair hair away

from her face. 'What was the matter with her? Why did she fall down like that?'

'Something to do with an infection that's started in her liver,' Ellen shook her head sadly. 'They'll let us know as soon as she's well enough to have you over to visit. In the meantime,' she smiled, 'what about a bit of breakfast?'

'Hmm, I'm not very hungry,' said Jenny, who felt an emptiness gnawing in the pit of her stomach that wasn't hunger. Then she remembered her promise to Carrie. She didn't expect Carrie would be feeling very hungry this morning, either. But if she had been well enough, Carrie's choice would have been a heap of creamy scrambled eggs piled high on a piece of soggy toast. 'Actually, Ellen,' she said, 'I *am* hungry! Can I have scrambled eggs on toast?'

Ellen arched her eyebrows in surprise. 'Really? Is that what you feel like? It's unlike you to have such an appetite in the morning!' She chuckled. 'I'll put the kettle on too. Come through when you're ready.'

Jenny got off the sofa and stretched. 'OK. Now, Jess, I'll have a wash and change, then I'll take you for a long walk.' At the mention of the word 'walk', Jess's plumy tail began to wag furiously.

Jenny squared her shoulders. A promise was a

promise. She was going to be as good as her word.

Jenny finished her mug of tea at the kitchen table and kept Ellen company whilst she washed up the breakfast things.

'There's a car coming up the drive,' Ellen said, plunging the small saucepan coated with sticky scrambled egg into the washing-up bowl. 'It's Anna MacLay . . . and Fiona! How nice.' She hurried to open the back door and the late June sunlight streamed across the flagstone porch.

'Have you time for a cup of coffee, Ellen? Hello, Jenny!' Mrs MacLay called.

Jenny went out to the top step. She had brushed her hair into a ponytail and changed into clean jeans and a T-shirt. Her tummy felt huge with the big breakfast she had eaten. 'Hello, Mrs MacLay.' She smiled. 'Hi, Fi.'

Fiona hurried over and leaped up the steps, looking serious. 'How's Carrie? I rang her house last night and her mum said she wasn't very well again.' She stooped to put her arms round Jess's neck. But Jess was looking expectantly up at Jenny.

'I was just going to take Jess for a walk. Do you want to come with me and then we can talk as we go along?' Jenny suggested.

16

'OK,' Fiona said. 'Is it all right if I go out with Jess and Jenny for a bit, Mum?'

Mrs MacLay was sitting at the big pine table in the kitchen, whilst Ellen spooned coffee granules into two mugs. 'OK, but don't be too long, Fiona. We're on our way into Greybridge for a weekly shop,' she explained to Ellen.

Fiona followed Jenny out of the door. Jess bounded ahead as they headed up a steeply sloping rise towards the land that ran along the crest of Windy Hill, the hill from which the farm took its name.

Black-faced sheep grazed contentedly along the horizon and, away in the distance, Jenny could see an expanse of blue sea, the same colour as the sky. 'Poor Carrie!' she said, linking her arm through Fiona's. 'I went over to see her yesterday and she was sitting up doing a jigsaw puzzle. But, when she stood up, she collapsed!'

'Did she faint?' Fiona said, frowning worriedly.

'Not a faint, exactly. She just fell over. She's got an infection in her liver, or something, which is making her weak.' Jenny shook her head, feeling yesterday's sadness creep over her again.

They had reached a little track that wound along the fenced land given over to the grazing sheep. One or two of the bolder animals raised their faces and

JESS THE BORDER COLLIE

sniffed the air, trying to sense if they were in any danger from Jess; others scampered away and some bolted in panic.

The girls walked on until they came to a section of field earmarked for the ewes and their recently-born lambs. They sat down to watch as the still awkward animals tottered about on their thin, wobbly legs, bleating loudly. Jess dropped down, panting from his run. He was not a working dog, but his instinct was good, and he knew how to behave among sheep.

'Carrie looked . . . awful!' Jenny confided. 'She was all yellow and thin. Oh, Fi, what are we going to do if Carrie *dies*?' Jenny covered her face in her hands.

Fiona put her arm round Jenny's shoulders. 'She won't,' she said firmly. 'There must be something the doctors can do at the hospital to make her better.'

Jenny gave a great, shuddering sigh and Jess came a bit closer. He whimpered and Jenny stroked him.

'He always seems to know when you're sad,' Fiona said wonderingly.

Jenny nodded. She felt wretched and she knew the collie could sense it.

'I know I haven't always been a good friend to you,' Fiona went on. 'Especially at first. I was quite nasty at times. I suppose I was a bit jealous of you having Carrie and Jess, and everything . . .'

Jenny looked at Fiona. 'Go on,' she urged.

'Well, I'm really sorry about that now. And, I just wanted to say that if Carrie . . . you know . . . ever . . .' She broke off.

'Dies,' Jenny finished, in a whisper.

'Yes, dies . . . then I'll try to be as good a friend to you as she has been. OK?'

'Thanks, Fi.' Jenny turned and gave Fiona a hug. They sat together like that for a minute, not talking.

Jenny felt comforted. She pulled away. 'We'd better go back down, or your mum will be wondering where you are.'

The two girls stood up, brushing the grass from their jeans.

'Right,' said Fiona.

'Fi?' Jenny said. Her friend turned. 'Thanks,' Jenny said simply.

When Mrs MacLay and Fiona had gone, Ellen remembered to give Jenny a message. 'Oh!' she said, 'I forgot to say that David Fergusson rang when you were out with the dog. He wants you to meet him to go walking with Jess and Orla, after football practice this afternoon.'

'I don't know...' Jenny was hesitant as she filled Jess's water bowl. She felt too miserable to want to do anything much.

Ellen came over and smoothed Jenny's cheek. 'Go on, Jenny. It'll do you good to get out, and I'm sure it would take your mind off Carrie.'

Jenny looked over at Jess. He had curled up in his basket and was looking straight at her, his head to one side. It made Jenny giggle. 'Well, we don't have to ask Jess what *he* thinks of the idea!' she said. 'OK. I'll cycle over to the pitch and meet him there later.'

Jenny went upstairs to tidy her room. She put aside a few bits and pieces to take over to Carrie when next she visited her: a book she'd read that she knew Carrie would enjoy, and a few comics and some bubble bath she'd had for her birthday but not used. Then, whilst eating a sandwich that Ellen had brought her upstairs for lunch, she answered a letter she had had from Ellen's nephew, Ian, in Canada, and told him all about his aunt's wedding.

Later that afternoon, as Jenny cycled out of the gates to Windy Hill, she tried not to allow her thoughts to dwell on Carrie. Jess loped along at her heel, his tongue already lolling and the tips of his ears rising and falling with each stride. It had clouded over, a bank of grey cotton wool coming in from over the sea, accompanied by a light wind.

When Jenny reached the football ground, some half a mile beyond Dunraven, the farm where the McLays lived, the game was just ending. Jenny looked at the dirt-smeared clothes and bleeding knees of the players. She shook her head. She couldn't understand the appeal of football, though David would have argued passionately in favour of the sport.

She spotted her friend, his dark, curly hair damp from his exertion, and waved. Jess put his nose in Jenny's hand, and she looked down and followed the collie's gaze. Orla, David's Border collie, was lying in the shade of a tree, waiting for her master. Even at the distance they were, Jenny could see Orla's tail swishing from side to side along the closely cropped grass at the side of the pitch.

Jess sprang forward to greet Orla as Jenny wheeled her bike up to the tree and propped it against a low-lying branch. 'Hello, girl,' she said softly and dropped down beside her to give her a stroke. Orla tugged at her lead, which was looped round the trunk, trying to reach Jess. 'I'll untie you,' Jenny told her, 'but I'd better not let you go. If you go tearing onto the pitch looking for David I'll be in real trouble.'

When the coach blew the final whistle, David jogged up to where Jenny was sitting, a dog on either side of her. 'Phew! What a game! We won,' he said triumphantly.

'I saw,' said Jenny. 'Ugh, you're all filthy and smelly.'

'Well, I don't have to change to walk the *dogs*, do I?' David laughed.

'I suppose not,' Jenny wrinkled her nose. 'Just keep your distance from me!' she teased.

'Right. Have you locked your bike?' Jenny nodded. 'Good. You can leave it here and we'll get it on the way back,' David suggested.

Jenny got to her feet and both collies jumped up and began to prance about excitedly. 'Let's walk that way, away from the pitch. There are too many cars swarming around collecting the other players,' she said.

They walked towards the sea, to where the fishing village of Cliffbay nestled under the cliffs. Jenny's thoughts turned back to Carrie, lying in her bed somewhere down there, and marvelled again at her amazing courage. She was just about to tell David the news about Carrie when a car appeared, driving slowly across the grass, straight towards them.

'What's he doing?' David said, squinting at the driver. 'Why can't he use the road like everyone else?'

The man behind the wheel was frowning and Jenny saw his passenger laugh. 'Let's go over to the shelter of the trees,' she suggested, feeling a bit nervous about the approaching vehicle.

They began to jog, but the car, a blue Volkswagen, followed a short distance behind. Jess, Jenny noticed, had begun to growl in a menacing way. The hackles on the back of his neck were standing up. Orla seemed afraid rather than angry. She was slinking along, her belly low and her ears flat.

They reached the cover of the coppice and peered out at the car. It had pulled up and now the men were getting out. Jess began to growl even more loudly and Jenny put a hand on his head. 'Jess!' she hissed. She looked over at the football pitch. The crowd had dispersed, all the players having been picked up. There was no one was about.

'What *do* they want?' David asked Jenny. 'Perhaps they are foreign . . . and lost. I'll go and find out—'

But at that moment, the men began to run straight towards them. Jenny clutched at David, her stomach lurching with fear. 'No!'

Jess barked fiercely, snapping his teeth in a way that scared Jenny. She couldn't remember ever seeing him behaving so aggressively.

David took a step backwards, and staggered. The

determined, leering faces of the men were bearing down on them. 'Run, Jenny,' he said. 'Run!'

3

Jenny's legs were paralysed with shock. Her brain told her that this could not be happening. It felt like a nightmare. Was it a joke? Had they been caught up in some kind of a play, being acted out on the green? Or was it a dream?

Her fingers curled into Jess's leather collar; his front feet were off the ground as he strained against her hold, his lips drawn back in a snarl. She heard David tell her to run, but Jess wouldn't move either. Jenny was frightened of letting him go – he might get hurt and she wanted him close beside her.

'Jenny!' David yelled. '*Move*, will you!'

Reluctantly, Jenny let go of the Jess's collar and he sprang forward, barking furiously. She turned and ran, following David as he ducked and dived under the low-hanging branches of the trees. She could hear his breath rasping as he ran. Her heart seemed to have slipped up into her throat. It thudded loudly in her ears.

It took only a moment before one of the men caught up with David. Jenny saw him reach out and seize her friend's upper arm, then, with a little jerk, David collided with the man's big body and fell against his legs.

Behind her, the other man was trying to fend off Jess. He had his leg outstretched, his big boot threatening to kick the collie in the chest. Orla was circling the man, snarling.

Jenny stopped, gripped by terror. 'Jess!' she screamed. The collie was holding his own, but a large cloth sack had been thrown over David's head. Jenny took shelter behind a tree, and peeped out. It had become clear that it wasn't her that the men wanted – it was her friend. David kicked out. She could see his muddy football boots flailing. His yells were muffled as he struggled inside the brown sack.

Pressed against the bark of the tree, Jenny gripped the trunk. Jess, with Orla close at his shoulder, had followed the other man to his car and had only just missed having his nose slammed in the driver's door. The blue car came jolting over the grass as David was pushed, stumbling towards it.

Not a word had been exchanged during the attack, but now, as Jenny watched her friend being shoved head-first into the back seat, the man who had caught him laughed. The driver revved the engine, and the car spun round and took off in the direction it had come.

'Jess! Here!' Jenny shouted, but the collie, usually so obedient, appeared not to hear her. His eyes were fixed on the back wheels of the car, and he began to chase it. Orla took her lead from Jess, looping around to join him as they bore down on their escaping quarry.

Realising she had to do something, Jenny hurried out from behind her tree and began to run after the car. Her legs felt like jelly and she was weak with fear. 'Stop!' she shouted. 'Jess! Come here! Oh, please . . . stop.' She could see Jess's speed hadn't faltered; he was keeping up well, while Orla, excited by the chase, was running alongside the driver's door.

Then, as the car slowed to negotiate a deep rut in

the ground, Orla drew level with the front of the car and sprinted round ahead of it. Just then the driver accelerated. Jenny heard a sharp yelp as the car struck her.

'Oh, no!' Jenny gasped. 'Orla! Orla!' She gathered speed, racing towards where the collie was lying. Having reached the road, the driver of the car put his foot down. The car tyres gripped the smooth tar and he headed easily out of sight.

Jess gave up his pursuit. He slowed, and came back to Jenny at a trot, his tongue dripping and his eyes wild with his exertion. He fell onto his side on the grass beside Orla, panting hard.

'Oh, Jess!' Jenny was relieved that the collie had returned safely to her. She dropped to her knees. 'Orla, are you hurt?' She ran her fingers gently down Orla's silky sides, feeling for a wound. She expected to feel the warm stickiness of blood, but found none. The collie lifted her head, and looked at Jenny with a bewildered expression in her eyes. Jenny smoothed her heaving sides, as Orla winced and whined.

'Oh, you *are* hurt. Poor girl!' Jess eased himself next to Orla. Jenny put a hand out to him. 'Good boy,' she said. 'You tried to protect us. You tried to help.' Then Jenny had a sudden thought. The puppies! She put her hand softly on Orla's belly. What if they had been

damaged by the blow of the car?

Jenny jumped up and looked around for someone who might help her. The green was deserted. Jess got up, his tail wagging slowly, and Orla struggled to get to her feet. The effort was too much for her. She yelped again and lay back. 'You stay here, Orla,' Jenny told her anxiously. She made a quick decision. She would leave Jess with Orla and cycle home for help.

Jenny took a deep breath to try and calm herself. Now was not the time to think about where the men had taken David, or what they might do to him. It was like an unfolding nightmare but, Jenny reasoned, there was nothing she could do immediately to help David – not until she got back to Windy Hill. And if she hurried, she might save the lives of Orla's puppies.

'Stay, Jess,' Jenny commanded. 'Wait there with Orla. I'll go home and bring Dad or Matt. Stay!' Jess cocked his head at his mistress, his tail still. Then he sat down, close to where Orla was lying. 'Good boy.' And Jenny started to run towards the tree where she had left her bike.

She willed herself to stay calm and wheeled the bike out of the coppice, steering it around the jutting roots of the trees. Her eye was caught by something smooth, shiny and yellow-brown in colour, lying among the bracken. Jenny snatched it up and turned it over quickly in her hand. It was a wallet, made of reptile skin. There was no time to inspect its contents, so she stuffed it into the pocket of her jeans, jumped on the bike, and pedalled as fast as she could for Windy Hill.

Matt was out in the cobbled yard, grooming his horse, Mercury, when Jenny skidded to a halt just inside the gates of the farm. It had begun to rain, a light, misty sort of drizzle that had settled on Jenny's eyelashes and made it difficult for her to see. She left her bike on the ground and began to run towards the house.

'Matt!' she shouted. 'Quick . . . I need help.'

Her brother looked up, surprised. 'What is it?' he said. He was tall in his riding-boots and, with his dark hair, looked very like their father, Fraser Miles. He held the grooming brush in one hand, and was gaping at his sister in obvious confusion.

'David's been taken away by two men and Orla got hit by their car. I think her puppies are hurt . . .' Jenny babbled, tugging at Matt's sleeve.

Matt blinked and was about to speak when Jenny, infuriated by his slowness, interrupted. 'Oh, Matt!' she shouted. 'Don't just *stand* there! Do something!'

She dashed off into the house, yelling: 'Dad! Ellen!'

For once, Fraser Miles was not up in one of the farm's distant fields. He was in the kitchen, pulling a nail out of his boot with a pair of pliers. Jenny could have kissed him she was so glad to see him. Her chest was aching with the effort of her running and her terrified heart still pounded in her ears.

'Dad!' she sobbed, and her father dropped the boot he was holding and came quickly to her side.

'What, Jenny? What is it? Is it Carrie?' Fraser held his daughter against his chest, stroking her hair with the palm of his hand.

'Two men forced David into a car down on the green and drove off with him. Orla was hit by the car as they drove away – I think she's . . . hurt!' Jenny said, explaining it as clearly as she could.

Ellen appeared from the utility room next to the kitchen, a frown on her face and an incredulous look in her eyes. Then Matt rushed in from the yard. Jenny was made to sit down and tell the story from the beginning, ending with her decision to leave Jess and Orla on the green.

'But this is . . . very hard to believe,' Fraser Miles said slowly, shaking his head.

'I'm not making it up – any of it,' Jenny said crossly. She stood up. 'I want to go back to the dogs, Dad.'

Ellen put her hand over Jenny's. 'We don't think you're making it up. Not at all.' She smiled encouragingly. 'And Jess will be fine there, for a while. You know how obedient and intelligent he is.'

'This just seems incredible . . . Who would have thought it?' Matt said. 'Right here in sleepy old Graston – a kidnapping!'

'Fiona always said there was something strange about David and his father. She thought they were criminals. Remember when Mr Fergusson called David *Douglas* once?' Jenny remembered, in a small voice. 'Poor David – he must be really frightened. I wonder if those men will hurt him?'

'Yes, well, better not to dwell on that right now.' Mr Miles said. 'I think we had better ring the police.' He went to use the telephone in the hall. Ellen slipped an arm round Jenny and squeezed her shoulder.

Jenny looked up at her pleadingly. 'But . . . Orla! We must get Mr Palmer to look at her, Ellen. She's hurt!'

'But there isn't any sign of a wound, you say?' Matt asked.

'No, but . . .'

'Shh!' Ellen hushed them while her husband began to speak to the police.

'Yes, Fergusson, that's right,' he was saying. 'Simon – and the son is David. About an hour ago – out on Parson's Green, the football pitch. The car? Hang on a minute, please.' He looked at Jenny and raised his eyebrows inquiringly.

'Blue,' she said. 'Um . . . a hunched-over little car – the one that looks like an insect.'

'Volkswagen beetle,' Mr Miles said into the telephone. 'Blue. No, we didn't get the registration, sadly.'

Jenny felt a pang of regret. She had been in a such a flurry of fear she hadn't even thought to look at the registration number of the car. Now she hadn't a clue to give to the police, except perhaps a vague description of what the men had looked like.

'Thank you, officer. We'll be waiting.' Fraser Miles replaced the receiver and came back into the kitchen. 'They're going to come up to Windy Hill. They'll want to take a statement from you, Jenny lass.'

'How long will they be, Dad? I've got to get back to the dogs – and get Orla to the vet. I can't hang about . . .' Jenny was agitated. She couldn't help thinking that the men might come back to get their revenge on Jess for trying to attack them. She knew that Jess wouldn't leave Orla. He had been told to stay – and stay he would, no matter what.

'They'll get here as soon as they can, but they haven't got anyone available to come out to us right this minute. Matt, can you drive your sister back down to the green? Ellen, will you help? Take a blanket for the dog. I'll ring Tom Palmer and tell him you'll call in at the veterinary surgery.' Jenny's father was brisk. A worried frown creased his forehead.

'Yes, of course,' Ellen said, snatching up a jumper from the back of a kitchen chair. 'I'll get some water for the dogs, and a bowl . . .' She hurried about the kitchen, filling a plastic squash bottle with cold water and screwing on the cap.

Jenny thrust her hands impatiently into her jeans pocket. She was desperate to get back to Jess and Orla. Just then, her hand came into contact with something smooth and cold. 'Oh, I found this, Dad . . .' She pulled it out. 'Near the place where those men took David.' Jenny put the wallet on the kitchen table.

'A wallet!' Fraser Miles opened it. 'Well, this should give us something to go on, if, that is, it belongs to the kidnappers. Go on, you three go and get the dogs. Hurry now, and I'll be waiting here with the police, when you get back.'

Jenny took the outside stairs at a single leap. 'Hold

on, Orla,' she said under her breath. 'I'm coming.'
And please, she prayed to herself, *don't let those puppies be harmed!*

4

The rain was falling steadily as Matt steered the pick-up in the direction of Cliffbay. Jenny sat in the front between her brother and Ellen, peering eagerly out of the window for a glimpse of the two collies.

'We should have brought a towel,' Ellen said, 'The dogs will be soaked in this weather.'

'There's plenty of rags and things in the back, under the old tarpaulin,' Matt said. 'We can use those.'

Jenny was silent. She still couldn't believe that David had been grabbed, right before her eyes, by two normal-looking men, and in broad daylight. Perhaps, she reflected, they meant to demand a ransom from Mr Fergusson in return for his son's life – but, no, that just seemed too fantastic to even think about.

'I wonder if Mr Fergusson is rich?' she asked out loud.

Ellen looked puzzled. 'I shouldn't think so. Not especially. Why?'

'I was just wondering if those men had taken David in order to get some money out of Mr Fergusson,' Jenny said.

'There are plenty of wealthy farmers around these parts who'd make better pickings than the Fergussons,' Matt reasoned. 'This kidnapping just doesn't make sense.'

'That's what I think.' Jenny was puzzled.

They had reached the football pitch and Matt slowed the pick-up. As it lurched up onto the grass verge he braked. From there the ground sloped away, before levelling out, then rising again to the crest where the coppice stood, shrouded in a misty cloak of rain.

Jenny gave a shout. 'They dogs are still there! Oh, thank goodness. Quick, Matt,' she urged. 'Try and get a bit closer, will you?'

'I don't want us to get stuck in the mud,' Matt muttered, as he slowly accelerated. 'That would be disastrous.'

Jess turned his head as they approached, and recognising the pick-up stood up and wagged his tail hard.

'Jess!' Jenny climbed over Ellen's legs and jumped out. Jess barked happily, but he didn't leave Orla's side. She had raised her head, her ears pricked. In spite of the coolness of the driving rain, the injured collie was panting.

Ignoring the water that dripped from her hair onto her cheeks, Jenny hugged Jess, congratulating him again and again for having obeyed her instructions so faithfully. The collie's thick coat was wet through and he shook himself vigorously, sending a shower of droplets into her face.

The other two clambered out of the pick-up and hurried over. Matt knelt next to Orla and began to examine her. He moved his hands cautiously over the dog, probing as gently as he could.

'She's not getting up, Matt,' Jenny said anxiously. 'Look, she can't move!'

'Well, I'm not a vet,' Matt said, dashing the rain out his eyes with the back of his hand. 'But I'd say she's broken a rib or two, from the feel of things.'

'Oh, gosh! The pups?' Jenny asked. 'Will they—?'

'I don't know, Jen,' Matt said kindly. 'Let's lift her into the truck and get her to Tom Palmer straight away.'

Ellen's dark hair was plastered to her scalp. She crouched on the muddy ground beside the collie, stroking and soothing her. 'There, you're a good girl. You're going to be just fine.'

Jenny was really grateful that Ellen had come along. She was so level-headed and kind.

Between them, Matt and Ellen managed to slide a blanket under Orla's body, making a sling to carry her to the pick-up. Jenny tried to keep Orla calm, but she struggled and whimpered, evidently fearful of the swinging motion of the makeshift hammock.

When Orla settled in the back of the truck, Jess jumped in, and Jenny made herself comfortable next to them, pulling the tarpaulin over herself and the two dogs. She picked through a pile of rags and decided against using them as towels. They were oil-smeared and smelly.

'Jen, come and sit in the front with us,' Matt urged.

Jenny's head popped out from under the tent she had made for warmth. 'No, I'll stay with the dogs. Drive as quickly as you can, Matt, please!'

★ ★ ★

The waiting-room in Tom Palmer's veterinary surgery was crowded with pet owners and their animals, but Orla was hurried straight through to the surgery examination room where Mr Palmer and his nurse lifted her gently onto the table.

'Your dad rang me, Jenny,' Mr Palmer began, 'so I have an idea what this is all about.'

Jenny nodded, and slipped her hand into Ellen's as Orla began to whimper. She had every reason to trust Tom Palmer – he had performed the operation on Jess that had straightened his damaged leg. She watched as he checked Orla's gums and the rims of her eyes.

'Well, she's a nice healthy pink, so she's not bleeding internally – that's a good sign,' he smiled. Then he listened to Orla's heart and lungs with a stethoscope. 'And no sign of any damage to the organs, either.'

Orla cowered on the smooth surface of the table, her head low and her tail tucked tightly between her legs. The room smelled strongly of disinfectant and other animals. She looked imploringly at Jenny.

When Mr Palmer moved his hands over her ribcage, she yelped sharply. 'Fractured ribs, I expect,' he said. 'Poor girl.'

'What about her puppies, Mr Palmer,' Jenny

breathed. 'Will they be all right?'

'I should think so, Jenny, but I'm afraid there is no way of knowing at this stage. We'll have to wait until she's ready to have them, in, say, about a week's time?'

Ellen nodded. 'That's about right,' she said.

'I'll give her something for the pain.' Mr Palmer prepared his syringe, then went on, 'My advice is that she is kept as quiet as possible. It might prove difficult for her to give birth with a couple of broken ribs – she may need a Caesarean operation when the time comes. But we'll wait and see.'

'Thanks, Mr Palmer,' Jenny said.

'Let's move her gently back to the pick-up, now,' he said. 'Left alone, those ribs will sort themselves out.'

'Matt will help . . . he's out in the truck, with Jess,' Jenny said. 'I'll go and get him.'

Orla seemed relieved to be back in the truck. She lay on her good side on the blanket, and twitched her tail gratefully when Jenny climbed in beside her. Rainwater had pooled in places in the open back of the pick-up, and as Matt drove away from the veterinary surgery it began to slosh about.

'Ugh!' said Jenny to Jess, who was pressed up against her. 'This is awful.' She was shivering in her damp clothing, and couldn't remember when she had last eaten. She closed her eyes, her arm supporting Orla, pushing out of her mind all the worry about the unborn puppies and David, and thought instead about a steaming mug of creamy hot chocolate.

When they reached the track leading to the farm, Jenny looked out from under the tarpaulin, expecting to see a police car. She held on to Orla, trying to shield her from the lurching of the pick-up as Matt negotiated the muddy and rutted road to the house. There was no sign that the police had come to Windy Hill – not even a lone policeman's bicycle was in evidence.

'They haven't come!' Jenny said indignantly, as Ellen got out of the cab and came round to the back. 'And David is in real *danger*!'

'I'm sure they'll be here soon,' Ellen said reassuringly. 'Let's go inside and ask your father . . . there might be news.'

Warmth from the big range in the farmhouse kitchen lifted Jenny's spirits. She kicked off her soaking shoes, and Ellen did the same.

'Make way!' called Matt, as he carefully eased himself through the door with Orla in his arms. 'She's heavy – and those ribs will be tender.'

'Put her down next to the Aga,' Ellen suggested.

Matt lay Orla on a blanket Jenny had placed there. The collie was looking very sorry for herself. Jess went over and inspected her, sniffing at her coat curiously, and particularly at the spot on the back of her neck where she had had her injection. Then, he went and drank from his water bowl.

'Dad!' Jenny called.

'Fraser – we're back,' Ellen was at the bottom of the stairs. But there was no answering shout from the top floor of the house.

Matt had flopped into a chair and was using his

handkerchief to wipe his wet face. 'He can't have gone out, surely? Wasn't he going to wait in for the police?'

'That's what he said,' Ellen looked puzzled.

Jenny, whose head was filled with the strange confusion of the last few hours, suddenly gasped. 'Oh! Ellen! You don't think the men have come back and . . .' But the slamming of the back door stopped her and she turned to see her father kicking off his wellington boots in the kitchen porch.

'Dad!' She ran to him. 'Any news?'

'Ah, you're back, lass. The dog all right?' Fraser, too, was wet through, and slightly out of breath.

'She's broken a couple of ribs, poor girl,' Matt said.

'Mr Palmer doesn't know if the puppies have been hurt,' Jenny added. 'He says we'll have to wait and see. Did you ring Mr Fergusson?'

'I tried – no reply, I'm afraid.' Fraser put an arm round Ellen, then sat down. 'I had to go out. Callum MacLay came over to say that our ram had got out of the top field.' Jenny's dad shook his head and sighed. 'What a job I had trying to catch him!'

'Oh, Fraser!' Ellen was dismayed. 'Not again!'

'Yes. The hikers have weakened the wall by climbing it, I think. And someone had removed the flat top stone and put it into the field to use as a handy picnic table! So the ram had an easy escape route.'

'How did Mr MacLay spot Sam?' Matt asked.

'That cheeky ram came over onto Callum's land – looking for the ewes, I expect!' Fraser Miles chuckled.

'Sam is safely back behind the wall now, I take it?' Ellen smiled.

'He is, thankfully,' Mr Miles yawned. 'Any chance of a good, strong cup of tea, Ellen?'

'Or a cup of hot chocolate?' Jenny put in hopefully.

'Why don't you and Matt go and change your clothes Jenny, and I'll do the same. Then, we'll turn our thoughts to something to eat and drink, all right?'

'Good idea,' said Matt and Jenny together.

Jenny was first down into the kitchen and took the chance to spend a little time with Jess. He was curled up in his basket, snoozing, but wagged his tail when she came over.

'Hello, boy,' she said softly. 'What a day it's been!' She sat down on the floor beside him. Orla was fast asleep and didn't stir.

Jess lifted a paw and put it on Jenny's arm. He looked at her steadily, his brown eyes fixed on hers while she stoked his ears and the top of his head, then she took his paw in her hand. 'Good dog,' she told him. 'Clever boy.'

She noticed a smudge of blood on her bare forearm. Quickly, she turned Jess's foot and looked at the pad. The leathery skin was scored by gravel-filled cuts, one of which was still bleeding.

'Oh, Jess! You're hurt!' Jenny cried, and examined each foot in turn. The back feet were less affected, but Jenny guessed that the lacerations under the front feet had been caused by the collie's frantic dash along the tarred road after the speeding car that had taken David away.

Jenny brought over a twisted strip of raw hide for Jess to chew. He accepted it with a gentle mouth. While he was busy, she cleaned out the cuts by soaking each of his feet in a bowl of warm water. The gravel floated free and the water turned pink and brown.

'What are you up to?' Ellen was peering over Jenny's shoulder into the muddy, bloody bowl.

'I'm cleaning his feet. I hadn't realised he had been hurt when he sprinted along the road after David,' she replied.

'You're doing a great job there, Jenny,' Ellen said approvingly. 'I'll give you a little antiseptic ointment when you're finished, if you like.' She put the kettle on and took out a loaf of brown bread.

'The police are here, Ellen,' Matt announced, coming down the stairs. 'I saw the car from my bedroom window.'

'Oh, good.' Jenny was relieved. 'About time! Those horrible men are probably in Cornwall by now!'

5

Matt showed the police officers into the sitting-room. From the kitchen, Jenny could hear him making the introductions and her father politely thanking them for coming.

'I'll tidy up in here,' Ellen said, as she surveyed the puddles on the floor. 'You go and tell the police what you know. I'll join you in a minute or two.'

'Thanks, Ellen.' Jenny stroked Jess. 'You stay there, boy, and rest!' The collie climbed into his basket, turned in a circle and settled with a big sigh. Jenny stood up and took a deep, calming breath, feeling her tummy rumble at the same time. The sky outside was now a brooding dark grey and rain pattered relentlessly against the windows. She longed for good news, something to eat – and for the terrible events of the day to be over.

'Hello,' she said shyly, from the sitting-room doorway. A tall, young officer stood with his back to the small fireplace, which was filled with a basket of dried flowers. He had his cap tucked under his arm and he was examining the wallet she had found near the coppice on the green.

He looked up and smiled. 'Hello, there. You must be Jenny Miles?'

'Yes,' Jenny replied.

The second officer, an older man with a white moustache, was sitting beside Matt on the sofa.

'It sounds as though you've had a frightening day, Jenny,' he commented.

'Less frightening for me than for my friend . . . David,' she said. She perched on the arm of the big chair her father was sitting in and he took her hand in his.

'You've been a brave lass, Jen,' he said quietly.

'Yes,' the young policeman agreed, nodding. 'I'm PC Tim Lucas, by the way, and my colleague is PC

Alex Reece. Your father has filled us in briefly on what happened out on Parson's Green this afternoon. Are you able to tell us what these men looked like, Jenny?' He spoke gently, and Jenny found herself feeling less nervous.

'Well, they were very . . . ordinary looking,' she said. 'I didn't really get a chance to look *very* carefully, because we were trying to run away . . . and then I hid behind a tree.' Jenny looked up as Ellen slipped quietly into the room.

'This is my wife, Ellen,' Fraser Miles said. Ellen smiled and sat down.

'Go on, Jenny,' PC Lucas said.

'Um . . . one was quite tall, with sort of long, dark hair – straight hair . . .' Jenny was struggling. There didn't seem to be any distinguishing feature that she could describe. Then she had a sudden recollection of something she had seen while David was struggling inside the hessian sack. A flash of gold. 'That's it!' she said. 'An *earring* – quite a big, dangling loop. The man who pushed David into the sack was wearing it.'

PC Reece's pencil had been poised above a small notepad and now he began to write. 'Well done,' he said. 'That's the sort of information we need.'

'Do you have any idea where they could possibly

have taken David?' Jenny asked, adding: 'Will you be able to rescue him?'

'We have got a pretty good idea who these men are.' PC Lucas had turned to face Mr Miles. 'They're two members of a large syndicate of international criminals who mastermind the smuggling of skins and endangered animals into this country.'

'Really!' Matt's eyebrows had shot up. 'Big time stuff, then?'

'Yes.' PC Reece nodded grimly. 'A nasty bunch, indeed.'

'But why take David?' Ellen put in, puzzled. 'What's he got to do with endangered animal skins?

'It's an attempt, we believe, to get to his father, Mr Simon Fergusson,' the officer explained.

'What's he done – David's father, I mean?' Jenny asked, her voice barely above a whisper. If Mr Fergusson *was* a criminal, then Fiona's – and her own – early suspicions would have been correct. If his father had to go to jail then David, whose mother had also died, would be left all alone. Jenny was already deciding that David would live with them, at Windy Hill, when PC Lucas spoke up.

'Mr Fergusson is innocent,' he said. Jenny let go of the breath she had been holding. The officer went on: 'He's been under police protection for several months now.'

PC Reece took up the story: 'When Mr Fergusson lived in England, with his late wife and son, he was employed as an inspector for the RSPCA. It was he who stumbled across the work of this gang and reported it. Their ringleader was arrested, as a result, and was jailed,' he explained.

'So, now the rest of the gang are after Mr Fergusson?' Matt suggested.

PC Lucas nodded slowly. 'It seems they have successfully traced him to Graston – and have taken his son as an attempt to get to him.'

Matt whistled. 'This is like something you'd see on telly!'

'Why do they *want* Mr Fergusson?' Jenny asked, puzzled. 'What are they going to do with him?'

'They want to . . . stop him,' PC Reece said gently. 'You see, there is a big trial coming up in court in England. They don't want Mr Fergusson's evidence to be heard. He knows too much. What he has to say could bring in the whole of the gang, many of whom are in South America.'

Jenny looked across at her father. He was rubbing his eyes, as if in disbelief. 'How on earth could we have got mixed up with this . . . madness?' he asked, looking at Ellen and shaking his head.

'What are you going to do now?' Jenny prompted, looking from one police officer to the other. 'Do you *know* where they've taken David?'

'No,' PC Lucas said. 'Not yet. We'll take a few more details from you, Jenny, then, with the information we have from the wallet you handed in, we'll soon have several officers out on the trail. Don't you worry.' He winked at her and smiled, but Jenny didn't feel very reassured. Hours had passed since David had been taken from the green – anything could have happened to him.

'Will they . . . hurt David?' she asked.

'Not likely!' PC Reece blustered. 'If they're trying to lure his father to where they're taken the boy, then David is worth keeping in good health, don't you think?'

Jenny nodded. *Poor David*, she thought for the second time that day. *He must be absolutely terrified.*

PC Lucas loomed over her, his notebook in his hand. 'Now, Jenny,' he said, 'I want you to tell me everything that happened this afternoon. Starting from the very beginning. All right, lass?'

When the police had finally gone, Jenny checked that Orla was sleeping peacefully, then sank wearily onto a kitchen chair. She put her chin in her hands. 'Phew! They asked so many questions!'

'They have to be sure of the details,' Matt said, helping Ellen carry the plates to the table.

'I suppose so.' Jenny yawned and looked out of the window. The low-hanging cloud had lifted and, as the sun slid slowly into the west, the sky turned a pretty apricot pink. Night was approaching – Jenny felt a little shiver of fear as she thought about David, out there, somewhere, alone.

'I've just tried Simon Fergusson again,' Mr Miles said, coming into the kitchen. 'No reply from the bungalow. I wonder where he's got to?'

'Well, the police are trying to contact him too,' Ellen reasoned. 'He's bound to turn up sooner or later.'

Jenny took a large helping of sliced cold meat and salad, some new potatoes and brown bread. 'Well I'm *starving*!' she said apologetically, when Matt raised his eyebrows at her.

'I'll make you that hot chocolate later, Jenny, I promise,' Ellen said.

'I hope Sam hasn't gone romancing the neighbourhood ewes again.' Fraser Miles grimaced as he speared a small, buttery potato. 'You'd think that wretched ram would be satisfied with the large number of ewes he has at his disposal here at Windy—'

Mr Miles was interrupted by a loud knocking on the back door. He pushed back his chair and hurried to answer it.

'Oh, *now* what?' Ellen said, looking perplexed.

Jenny saw David's dad step into the back porch. He was a head taller than her father, and strongly built, but, somehow, to Jenny, he looked as though he had shrunk since she had last seen him. His shoulders drooped, his head hung sadly and the expression on his face was extremely grim as he followed Fraser Miles into the kitchen.

'Hello,' Mr Fergusson said. 'Oh, I'm sorry to interrupt your meal – but I've just had a call from the police.'

At the sound of his voice, Orla raised her head and Jenny watched her wag her tail in welcome. The injured collie made no attempt to get up, but Jess wandered over sleepily to greet Mr Fergusson.

'I see you've got Orla here – thanks,' Mr Fergusson said.

Ellen stood up, pushing her plate away from her. 'We're so sorry about David. You must be very worried. Can I get you something? A drink?'

'No, thanks.' Mr Fergusson's skin was ashen. 'I really came to explain a few things—' he broke off. Lines of worry furrowed his brow. 'You've heard nothing further, have you?'

'I'm afraid not,' Ellen spoke for all of them. 'But the police have been here and they seem very certain that they'll be able to find these men.'

Fraser Miles pulled a chair up to the table and gestured for Mr Fergusson to sit down. He sank wearily into it.

'I blame myself, Fraser,' he said bitterly. 'I should have told the boy the whole truth. I should have seen to it that he was better protected. I failed him.'

'No,' Ellen said gently. 'You had no reason to think that this gang were going to trace you here to Scotland, Simon.'

'Also,' Matt put in, 'you *have* been under the protection of the police. You must have felt that you and David were safe.'

'So the police have filled you in on the background?' Mr Fergusson sighed. 'Perhaps I should have made David more aware of the situation – instead of just telling him half-truths. Then all this might have been avoided.'

'Do you mean,' Jenny asked, her eyes wide, 'that David doesn't *know* about why you're really living here in Graston – and about the gang of criminals and everything?'

'He knows to a certain extent.' Mr Fergusson sighed, again, more heavily. 'But I thought the less he knew, the better. He had enough to cope with after the death of his mother. I simply told him that, for reasons to do with home but which I couldn't explain yet, we had to move and we would have to change our names – and that the less we talked about the past the safer we would be.'

Jenny watched with pity as he wearily rubbed his eyes. 'Teale's our name, actually,' he went on. 'I'm Robert Teale and David is really Douglas, you see . . .' he trailed off, and sighed again, shaking his head. 'The police advised a change of identity because this particular gang operates on such a wide scale.'

'Poor boy,' Ellen said sympathetically. 'What a time it's been for him . . . for you both!'

'Yes,' Mr Fergusson agreed, adding, 'I suppose David just accepted the name-changes and the move because he was so upset at the time – he probably just thought of it as some sort of bewildering time when everything in his life was changing. He trusted me to know best. I feel awful now that I didn't explain everything to him. I thought I was doing the right thing.'

So that would explain the note I found a few weeks ago, pinned to the Fergussons' front door and addressed to Douglas, Jenny thought to herself She felt, in some small way, relieved. David's reluctance to tell her the reason for his father's unexplained absences from Graston made sense to her now. It wasn't that he didn't consider her trustworthy – but that he was confused and frustrated himself. 'Will you go back to using your real names now?' she asked.

'Best not, yet, I think, Jenny,' David's father replied. 'We'll stick to the names we're known by here until this whole nasty business is properly cleared up.'

'Seems sensible,' Fraser Miles put in.

'David's a bright boy,' Mr Fergusson went on. 'He must have worked most of it out for himself. He's kept his word and not talked about his life in England, before we moved here. But he hasn't asked me any questions.'

'It makes sense now,' Jenny nodded, 'why David has been so quiet and secretive.'

'What exactly is this syndicate of criminals up to, Mr Fergusson?' Matt asked.

'Capturing and slaughtering animals for their skins, for export,' he replied. 'Mostly the skins of endangered animals – caymans, snow leopards, cheetahs, those sort of animals. I used to work for the RSPCA, you see. One day there was a report that a German shepherd dog had trapped itself in a disused yard in south London and I went in after it. The dog was frightened and ran from me, finally squeezing through a small gap into a derelict building. I broke in – and found the gang's plunder. I went back, with a video recorder, and got my evidence on tape.'

'Good for you!' Jenny said enthusiastically, disgusted that anyone could trade in animal skins. Jess had wandered to her side and put his nose affectionately into her lap. Jenny stroked his head, pleased that he didn't seem to be bothered by the cuts on his feet.

'I quite agree,' Fraser Miles added.

'It's what I believe in – protecting animals – but I never anticipated that it would put David's life in danger. Anyway,' Mr Fergusson shook his head, 'I'd better get back home in case the police need to contact me again.' He stood up. 'I just wanted to fill you in, really. And I'm glad you're all right, Jenny. Thanks for acting so quickly.'

'David would have done the same for me,' Jenny said seriously. 'And don't worry, they'll find David, I'm sure of it.'

'I hope you're right,' Mr Fergusson said. 'Listen, I'll keep in touch. Goodnight now.'

'Goodnight,' Ellen said. 'Take care.'

When Jenny had finished helping Ellen to clear the table and tidy the kitchen, she decided to telephone Carrie. Only a day had passed since she had witnessed her friend's collapse, yet it felt like a week – so much had happened in such a short space of time.

'You don't think it's a bit late to be phoning now?' Ellen wondered, looking at her watch.

'It's not nine o clock, yet,' Jenny said. 'I'm sure it'll be OK. I really want to talk to her and I'm sure she'll be glad of a chat.'

'OK,' Ellen shrugged and smiled.

Picking up the telephone, Jenny about thought how wonderful it would be if Carrie were able to come into school the following day. For a second, she allowed herself to imagine her friend as she once had been . . . her sunny, cheeky face, and the mop of unruly red hair, demanding that Jenny help her with her maths homework *quickly*, before the teacher arrived to start the lesson . . . And then she remembered that David wouldn't be in school the following day either and she felt a knot of fear twist in her stomach.

Pushing the thought to the back of her mind, she dialled Carrie's number. Mrs Turner answered straight away. Her voice sounded strained and anxious. 'Hello?'

'Hello, Mrs Turner. It's Jenny,' she said. 'Is Carrie feeling better now? Is she still up? Can I talk to . . .'

'Carrie's not here, Jenny,' Mrs Turner cut her short. 'She's back in hospital, I'm afraid.'

'Oh.' Jenny's heart turned over, adding to her feeling of anxiety. She couldn't think of anything sensible to say. 'Um . . . sorry I bothered you,' she said, in a small voice.

'Jenny?' Mrs Turner's voice was gentle. 'I'll let you know when you can visit, OK?'

'OK,' Jenny repeated woodenly. 'Thanks. Bye.' She

replaced the receiver and sank to the floor. The lights in the kitchen had been turned out. Jess's paws made a pattering sound as he came across to her and sat down next to her. Jenny wound her arms round his chest and back and buried her face in his fur. He smelled of rain and heather.

'Oh, Jess,' she said sadly, 'I can't bear it. I just can't bear it.'

6

Jenny's alarm clock startled her awake at six-thirty the following morning. She had an urge to snuggle up in her blankets and go back to sleep. That way, she would not have to think about Carrie, or David, or the possibility of Orla losing her puppies.

In the middle of a big stretch and simultaneous yawn, her bedroom door was eased open and Fraser Miles put his head round it.

Jenny sat up, surprised. 'Dad! How come you're not out on the farm?'

'I had a little lie-in this morning.' Her father grinned. 'Ellen spoilt me with breakfast in bed – and as Matt is leaving for college at lunch-time he offered to go out and do the work that needs doing.'

Jenny was suspicious. 'But you never miss your early-morning start.'

'I wanted to spend just a few minutes with you,' her father replied, sitting on the bed beside her. 'How are you?'

'How am *I*?' Jenny shrugged and wrinkled her nose. 'Well, I'm . . . healthy. So, I guess that makes me lucky.'

'But,' her father persisted, 'how are you feeling – inside?'

'Oh, up and down. I feel really positive one minute and scared and sad the next,' she said. Jenny smiled encouragingly at her father. He looked concerned and she didn't want to worry him.

'It's a tough time for you,' he stated. 'There's been a lot to cope with.'

'Yes,' Jenny said. 'I'm worried about David, and Orla's puppies, but mostly I'm worried about Carrie. I feel so helpless. She hates hospital . . . she hates the drugs and having no hair and being so sick . . . and I can't do anything to help her,' Jenny finished, frowning.

'You're doing all you can,' Fraser Miles took Jenny's fingers in his big, rough hands and squeezed them. 'You're being strong for Carrie. And that's that's the most important thing a friend could do.'

'Actually, I made her a promise,' Jenny said wistfully. 'I promised her that I would live life for her, and enjoy it for her too. That's what I'm really trying to do. But it's hard. It's hard to be without her, and to be cheerful.'

'I know it is,' Jenny's dad agreed. 'And I want you to know that I'm very proud of you.'

Jenny smiled at him and then became aware of the rhythmic thumping of a tail on wood. Jess's brown eyes looked lovingly at her from the door of the bedroom.

'Jess!' The collie took Jenny's greeting as an invitation and bounded into the room, grabbing a slipper as he did so. He presented it to Jenny by dropping it onto the bed and putting his nose gently into the palm of her hand.

'Now, that dog ought to know better. He is not supposed to be *upstairs* in the house . . .' Fraser Miles began, his tone playfully stern. Jess dropped to his haunches and began to ease himself gingerly under the bed.

Mr Miles threw back his head and laughed. 'All

right, Jess. Maybe just this once.' He winked at Jenny, knowing full well that there had been plenty of times recently when Jess had been sneaked into her bedroom for a cuddle. 'Maybe you can get her out of bed and off to school, can you?'

Jess sat up and his bright eyes seemed to be smiling at Jenny. She smoothed his silky ears and he licked her hand. 'I've always got you, Jess,' she said. 'Thank *goodness* I've got you!'

Jenny sat next to Fiona on the bus to school that morning. The swaying motion of the lumbering vehicle made her sleepy and her head soon began to nod.

'Hey, sleepyhead,' Fiona said, nudging her. 'You're flopping onto my shoulder.'

'Sorry.' Jenny yawned. 'I couldn't sleep last night, not very well, anyway.'

'Thinking about Carrie?' Fiona asked, her eyebrows coming together in a frown.

Jenny nodded. Fiona had also telephoned Cliff House and discovered that Carrie was back in hospital. But Jenny didn't dare let on what else she was worrying about. That morning, as she ate her cereal, her father and Ellen had advised her against talking about what had happened to David.

'Mr Fergusson will inform the headmaster, I expect, Jenny,' Mr Miles had said. 'We don't want everyone talking and making a fuss. It'll only make things worse.' Ellen had agreed with him and warned Jenny that if the newspapers in the district became involved, there would be no peace.

'You'll have news reporters snooping around for days,' she had said, with a shudder. 'They'll hound us for every tiny detail. Best not to say anything – remember it could put David in further danger.'

Jenny had promised, but her heart was heavy as she left for school. Jess had waited at the door after his breakfast for his usual morning walk up to the field before Jenny caught the bus. His tail wagged briskly, expectantly, but she had decided against taking him. The pads of his paws were still tender and when she gently prodded, he pulled his foot away sharply.

Orla had pottered around on the grass in the back garden, stepping hesitantly, like a dog grown suddenly very old. From time to time, she paused to lick the site of her injury, to soothe her obvious discomfort. Jenny had put her hands on the collie's tummy, feeling hopefully for signs of life. It felt warm and full, but beyond that she could feel nothing.

Now, lost in thoughts of Jess's mournful eyes as she

had left him in the kitchen, she spoke impulsively. 'Jess is desperate for a good walk.'

'Why?' Fiona asked. 'Didn't you walk him this weekend?'

Jenny flushed. 'Um . . . not as far as he would have liked, really.'

'Let's go after school today, then, shall we? I'll meet you on the cliff path.'

Jenny's friend was eager, so she nodded, not wanting to explain to Fiona about Jess's sore feet – hoping that the rest he'd had at Windy Hill during the day would mean he would be up to it.

'All right,' she said.

When they reached Greybridge Senior, Jenny heard the boys talking as they got off the bus. 'Good old Fergusson,' said one. 'He's managed to wangle a day off school to get out of doing his science test!'

'Nice one!' said another, and laughed.

Jenny wondered for the hundredth time where David was, and how he was being treated. A science test seemed like a positive comfort in comparison.

Jess was so keen for a walk when Jenny got home from school that she relented immediately. 'You win,' she laughed, as Jess pounced and pranced around her. 'But go easy on those poor old feet!'

'You'll take care, won't you, Jenny?' Ellen was putting some cut flowers from the garden into a vase. 'Stick to open places and the paths you know.'

'I will, Ellen,' she said. 'And, don't worry, I've got Jess to look after me.'

'Yes,' she agreed. 'I don't think I would be happy to let you go without him, so it's just as well his feet are on the mend.'

Jenny took a moment to check on Orla. The collie was dozing on her blanket, lying on her good side. She opened her eyes and blinked at Jenny but made no attempt to lift her head. 'Poor girl,' Jenny kissed her soft head, as Ellen brought over a bowl of milk for the collie.

'I'm trying to build her strength, but she seems to have very little energy,' she said with a frown.

'Do you think we ought to take her back to Mr Palmer?' Jenny asked.

'He advised us to let nature take its course,' Ellen shrugged. 'She'll heal — it'll just take time for the bones to knit.'

'Ellen, we haven't *got* much time, have we? I mean, before the puppies are born?' Jenny asked anxiously.

'Not really, no,' Ellen agreed, stroking Orla's smooth back. 'It won't be long. That is, if our calculations are correct.'

Jenny sighed. 'We just have to hope for the best,' she said, getting up off the floor. 'I'm going out now with Jess to meet Fiona.'

'Bye, love,' said Ellen.' Please take care, won't you?'

But Jess had already persuaded Jenny out of the door. She was racing along behind him, her spirits suddenly lifted by the fresh air and the exertion.

Fiona was waiting at their agreed meeting place. She gave Jenny a hug. 'You look better,' she announced. 'You were miserable at school today!'

Jenny wished she could share her burden of troubles with her friend, but she only smiled. 'I'm fine,' she grinned. 'Come on, let's go!'

Jess trotted ahead, pausing to examine the places that interested him. Fiona tucked her arm through Jenny's. 'I've decided,' she began, 'we're not going to talk about Carrie this afternoon. We're going to try and put her sickness out of our minds and enjoy the afternoon.'

'Right,' Jenny agreed, remembering her promise to Carrie. 'What shall we talk about?'

'Well, my having one of Orla and Jess's puppies, for a start!' said Fiona.

Jenny stopped. 'Really?' Her eyes were wide. 'Did your mum say you could?'

'No.' Fiona made a face. 'She says we've already got a dog and we can't have another. But Toby is Paul's dog. I'd like one of my own – one like Jess,' she finished.

'Maybe you'll persuade her,' Jenny smiled. She couldn't allow herself to worry about Orla's litter being born anything but strong and healthy. The arrival of a perfect puppy was too important to Carrie for fate to cheat her now.

It was nice walking along in the sunshine with Fiona. Jess seemed to be fine and not at all bothered by his damaged feet. They walked with their backs to the sea, sticking to the familiar track that wound its way along the cliff top, which was still tacky with mud from yesterday's rain.

But suddenly, Jenny noticed that Jess was behaving unusually. He had strayed some way from the path and was standing stock-still, one paw lifted, staring into the undergrowth.

'Jess! Here, boy,' Jenny called, walking towards him. The collie looked up, but didn't move. Instead, he began to bark loudly and paw at the ground.

'He's found something he wants to play with,' Fiona decided, following Jenny. Jess had managed to drag something from the tangle of ragwort and stinging nettle. He held it in his mouth and, as Jenny approached, dropped it at her feet.

'A can of Coke – empty!' Fiona said, smiling. 'What a pity, Jess. A cold drink is just what I feel like, too!'

The collie looked intently up at Jenny, barking sharply. He sniffed the dented aluminium can, rolling it over with his nose and smelling the underside of it. Then, while Jenny looked after him in puzzlement, he ran off into the trees, yapping all the while.

'What's up, I wonder?' Jenny turned to ask Fiona. Moments later, Jess tore back towards Jenny, barked insistently, then ran back to the thicket.

'You know him better than I do,' Fiona said, shrugging. 'It can't just be a rabbit, or a stray cat – can it?'

'No,' Jenny felt certain. 'No, for some reason, Jess is trying to get us to follow him.' The dog's nose was glued to the ground, like a hound on the scent of the fox. He was making it clear that he wanted Jenny to pay attention.

'Come on,' Jenny said suddenly. 'Let's go with him.'

'Um . . . do you think we should?' Fiona was hesitant. 'We're not supposed to go off the track we know, are we?'

'But this might be important,' Jenny said firmly. 'Come with me, Fi, please.'

'But . . .' Fiona looked uncertain. She pointed to the trees. 'We don't know where this leads.'

'We're not far from the road that runs along down to Cliffbay,' Jenny reasoned. She put out her hand as Jess approached her again, and took hold of his collar. 'What's the matter, boy?' The collie began to pull with all his strength, tugging Jenny in the direction he wanted her to go.

Jenny remembered her promise to Ellen to be careful and she hesitated. She might be leading Fiona into danger – and Fiona had no idea about David's plight. But Jenny's faith in Jess overruled the warning voice in her head. The collie was as tense as she had ever seen him, and determined to follow and investigate the scent he'd picked up on the Coke can. Jenny could hardly restrain him a moment longer.

'That's it,' Jenny said firmly. '*I'm* going with Jess. Are you coming?'

'Oh, all right,' said Fiona. 'I do trust Jess, but I hope this isn't just a wild-goose chase.'

Jenny shook her head. 'I'm sure it isn't. Go on, Jess. We're coming with you. Go on!'

The collie sprang ahead, pausing briefly to look back over his shoulder and make sure that Jenny was following. Then, nose to the ground, he took off.

7

Jess sprinted along through the bracken, leaping effortlessly over the hillocks of brush, and ditches full of stinging nettles. The girls jogged after him, heading away from the path they knew. The ground was rutted and difficult to cross and soon mud coated their trainers, making it difficult to grip the surface.

'Keep up!' Jenny urged Fiona.

'Can't you get him to slow down, Jen?' she grumbled. 'Why do we have to hurry like this?'

Jess darted this way and that, his nose quivering.

Once or twice he stopped, and lifted a paw, looking around as though he was thinking. Then he found a trace of the trail he was on, and he loped away again.

'Jess feels this is urgent!' Jenny explained. She hadn't seen her dog quite so solemn and so intent on anything before. He was on to something, and Jenny silently hoped that, somehow, he was going to lead her to David. After all, she reasoned, Jess had never let her down before.

'I don't know how much further I want to go, really, Jen. I mean, this . . .' Fiona had started to speak when Jenny saw Jess drop like a stone. He crouched there, his belly on the ground and his nose on his paws, panting, just the way Nell and Jake did when they were herding sheep.

'Shh!' She put a warning finger to her lips and glared at Fiona. She could see immediately that her friend was puzzled and a bit hurt. 'Sorry,' she hissed. 'I didn't mean to get cross. I'll explain everything to you in a while, OK? Just stay with me – and don't *talk*!'

Fiona's frown deepened but she followed Jenny's example and dropped to her haunches.

Up ahead of them, just visible through the trees, was a dilapidated shack, a half-ruined croft long since abandoned to the forces of nature. It had been pitched forward by the trunk of a tree growing close to its foundations, tilting it dramatically to one side.

As Jenny peered at the building from behind an overhanging fringe of leaves, she felt her mouth go dry. She gestured to Fiona to stay where she was. Jess hadn't moved. He was busily licking the underside of his front paw. It seemed that his job was done.

What do I do now? Jenny thought, feeling fear began to stir in the pit of her stomach. *I was crazy to come here*, she scolded herself. But then, the sound of a muffled shout came clearly to her ears.

'David!' said Jenny, looking at Fiona, her eyes huge.

'David?' whispered Fiona, whose hair had become entangled with the branches of a low-lying bush. 'Here? Have you gone completely mad?'

'It *is* David!' Jenny said triumphantly. 'This must be where the men have hidden him.'

Jess's ears were pricked and his head cocked to one side. He was listening intently. The shout came again, louder this time, tailing off into a weary sounding groan.

'David is at home, feeling poorly,' said Fiona, who was still staring blankly at Jenny. 'That's where *David* is. Um . . . we are talking about David *Fergusson*?'

Jenny crawled over to be closer to Fiona. 'Listen, Fi,' she said, speaking quietly. 'I'm not supposed to tell you any of this. David was kidnapped on Sunday from Parson's Green. The police are looking for him right now . . .'

'What?' Fiona's jaw dropped. She wrenched herself away from the grasp of the bush. 'Ouch!'

'I know it sounds as though I'm making it up but I'll tell you everything later . . .' Jenny said.

'Tell me now!' Fiona had seized Jenny's sleeve and was tugging at it.

'*Later!*' pleaded Jenny.

A long, low moaning sound reached them. Goosebumps broke out over Jenny's arms but Jess's tail had began to wag happily. 'You see!' Jenny hissed. 'It is David in there! It must be! Jess recognises his voice. Come on.'

Jenny crawled forward cautiously.

'Shouldn't we tell the police? He may be hurt . . . he'll need a doctor,' Fiona protested behind her.

'Come *on*,' Jenny said firmly. 'Come with me, Fi, *please.*'

Taking her lead from Jess, who had gone forward to the shack, Jenny approached a dusty window. She felt as though her heart was going to burst it was hammering so hard. Using her sleeve, she wiped at the outside of the pane, which was partly covered with ivy, leaving only a small, smeared space to look through. Years of dirt clung to the glass inside, and Jenny found herself peering in on a pile of rotting wood.

'See anything?' whispered Fiona, fearfully.

Jenny shook her head. She walked cautiously round the old croft, stepping over fallen timber as she went. The roof had collapsed in places and the walls were crumbling. But then, when she reached the far side of the building, she discovered a little room standing intact. Jenny guessed it had been a later addition to the place. On a heavy wooden door, a brass padlock was hanging, shining new in the bright sunshine.

Jenny knocked softly. She found herself breathing so hard that her chest was rising and falling, making her hand shake. Jess, beside her, nudged her with his nose and wagged his tail encouragingly.

'David?' she called softly. There was no answering sound.

'Here,' said Fiona, pointing, 'there's a knothole in the wood of the door, look.'

Jenny knelt and put her eye to the smooth, oval opening. She gasped. In spite of the gloom, she could clearly see David, his face towards her and his eyes closed. He was curled on his side on the floor. Jenny's heart somersaulted in her chest and she clutched at

Fiona. 'He's in there! He doesn't look . . . at all well.'

Fiona nudged her aside and put her face to the hole. 'Oh, gosh, Jen . . . he *is* alive, isn't he?'

'We heard him. He must be.' Jenny was desperate. Should she try and break down the door or run home for help? Her hands were clasped anxiously, her fingers twisting, when she saw Jess's ears go up. His body tensed and he looked up at Jenny and whined. Then the collie began to hurry away in the direction they had come, stopping once to look back pointedly at his mistress.

Jenny listened. 'There's a car coming!' she breathed. 'Quick, Fi, follow Jess.'

Putting her faith in Jess's good sense, Jenny grabbed Fiona's hand and followed the collie to where a water-worn ravine had been carved out across the land. A thin trickle of foul-smelling, brackish water flowed towards the sea. It had pooled in places, dammed by twigs and leaves and the odd bit of litter blown there by the wind. As Jess leapt into this gully, Jenny noticed a Coke can, dented like the one they'd seen before, bobbing in the water. Fiona hesitated only a second before she joined Jenny in the ditch.

'Oh, yuck!' she said. Her hands were smeared with mud, which had also travelled from her trainers up the lower half of her jeans. Then, looking at Jenny, she added in a whisper. 'I'm so scared my teeth are chattering.'

Jenny tucked her arm through her friend's and pulled her closer, to where a screen of fern leaves growing along the bank provided a scanty shield.

'Keep down,' she urged. 'We can see what's going on from here.'

Jess began a low, rumbling growl and his fur bristled. There came the slamming of a car door, then a second. Jenny put her hand softly on the back of Jess's neck, trusting that he wouldn't give the game away.

'You drink any more of that, Dylan,' said a voice, 'your teeth will rot.' Jenny raised her head a fraction, and peeped through the fronds. Two men had got out of a car – the same blue Volkswagen in which David had been driven away. One of them – Dylan, Jenny guessed – drained the last of his Coke and lobbed the can towards a tree. The big gold earring he wore jiggled.

'Nah,' he said, grinning. 'I ain't got my own teeth anyway, see, Ken?' To Jenny's disgust, he eased the false teeth away from the roof of his mouth, making them clatter, then laughed at his own joke.

'Yuck,' whispered Fiona again. Jenny glanced at

her and put a finger to her lips. Her friend was as pale as chalk, hunched in the ditch hugging her knees, a streak of mud across one cheek.

'Now,' said Ken, groping in the pocket of his baggy trousers and hauling out a big key, 'Let's see how our scrawny little friend is doing in here.'

'I got him beans,' said Dylan. 'Kids like beans, don't they?'

'Beans? You mean beans in tomato sauce? Didn't you bring him a sausage at least?' asked his friend.

'Nah. That kid's got no appetite anyway. He's too scared. Beans is fine.' As Ken unlocked the door to the shed, Dylan idly examined the label on his tin of beans. 'I remembered to bring the opener, too,' he remarked.

The door swung open smoothly, silently. Jenny stood up to get a better look. The hair at the back of her neck was wet with sweat but she felt cold, with fear as Fiona tried to tug her down again.

'Stand up, boy,' Ken was commanding loudly. 'Get to your feet. You need to eat. Come out.'

It was some moments before Jenny heard a shuffling sound. David emerged into the sunlight, blinking. His hands were tied behind his back and his ankles were roped together. Jess whimpered and cocked his head, not taking his eyes off David for a second.

Fiona squeaked. 'Oh, Jenny . . . *poor* David.'

It was obvious that David had been crying. His face was swollen and his eyes puffy. He limped along, his head drooping. He looked the picture of misery. *How dare these men treat him this way!* Jenny thought furiously. Anger surged through her, making her feel suddenly very hot.

Jess stiffened; he was ready to spring, but Jenny held his collar. 'No, Jess,' she warned.

Dylan opened the beans and thrust a spoon from his pocket into the tin. 'Here, boy,' he grinned. 'I got you a little treat.'

David shook his head. 'Why have you brought me here?' he demanded. 'Why can't I go home?'

Dylan and Ken cackled. 'Because you're our bait,' Dylan told him. 'You're the bait that's gonna catch us our fish, see?'

'Not long to go now either, I reckon.' Ken sniffed. 'We're soon gonna move you to a nicer place, see? A place where you can hear the sea, and the birds calling . . .'

'Are we?' Dylan looked surprised. 'Where's that then?'

'The boss said something about moving him down

to that wharf building he was telling us about.' He began to pick his teeth. 'You gonna eat them beans or not, boy?' he added nastily. David shook his head again.

'Don't waste my time!' shouted Dylan, aiming a kick at David's shin.

The open can of beans emptied onto the ground as Dylan's boot collided with David's leg. He gasped and tears began to slide down his cheeks.

Jenny looked at Fiona, horrified, and in that second, Jess slipped from her grasp and bounded out of the gully. 'Oh, no!' Jenny breathed.

Jess's hackles were up and his teeth bared. He growled threateningly as the men spun round in surprise.

'Jess!' sobbed David. 'Oh, Jess!'

'Looks like that mutt we saw yesterday, the one who was with the girl,' Dylan said, backing away.

'Same pesky animal, I reckon,' said Ken. 'The one we *didn't* manage to hit with the car.' He chuckled under his breath.

The two girls peered fearfully from the lip of the ditch. Jenny's heart was pounding in anguish as she watched her beloved dog crouching in front of the two men. The collie looked from one to the other, as though he was trying to size up the most efficient means of attack.

Then Jess made his decision. He raced round behind Dylan, coming in fast and low. Launching himself, he grabbed the fleshy bit of the man's thigh between his teeth and bit down, hard.

Dylan screamed and toppled over backwards. 'Brute!' he yelled. 'Get him, Ken, will ya?' He clutched the back of his leg.

Ken felt in his pocket once more, and this time he pulled out a knife. Jenny saw the glint of the long, sharp blade as it twisted in his hand. She stood up, but Fiona yanked her back down. 'Don't be *stupid*!' she begged Jenny. 'That man has got a *knife*!'

Jenny was breathing hard, her hands covering her mouth in terror.

'Jess . . .' she murmured. 'Oh, be careful.'

'You want a fight do you, doggie?' snarled Ken, as he squared up to the collie. 'Come on then . . . come on, good doggie. You come and get Ken.'

Jess crouched low, growling and prowling around the man like a lion closing in on its chosen prey.

'You know this dog, don't you, boy?' Dylan asked David. 'Do you want to see him die?'

Ken took a step towards Jess and raised his knife. It was poised to strike should the collie come any closer. But Jenny could take it no longer. With one swift leap she was free of Fiona and out of the gully, tearing towards the men, and David.

'Jess! Don't!' she screamed.

'Jenny!' David yelled.

Jess turned his head quickly as she came, and Ken plunged his knife down towards his spine. But the collie sprang aside in time and, with open jaws, went for Ken's arm.

'Aargh! You beast!' he yelled, dropping his weapon. His eyes were fixed on Jess, who was still circling menacingly.

'Ken, it's that girl. The one we saw on the green,' Dylan shouted.

Jenny, her whole body trembling violently, stooped and snatched up the knife, then began to back off. 'The police are on to you!' she shouted, beside herself with rage and fear.

'Now, we don't want no trouble, sweetheart,' Ken said, holding up his uninjured arm. His eyes flickered from the knife in Jenny's hand to the fierce, slavering jaws of Jess.

'Ken,' Dylan said, 'let's move out. This is getting too complicated. We don't want to involve no one else in this. No serious injuries, the boss said. Remember?'

'Call your dog off,' Ken said. 'Call him off, and we'll go.'

'All right,' said Jenny. She was dumbfounded at the effect she and Jess had had on the men. 'Here, Jess!' Could the men mean to free their prisoner?

Jess, still growling, went quickly to Jenny's side. She put a trembling hand on his collar. But to her dismay, she saw Dylan beginning to move David towards the car.

'Leave him!' Jenny shouted. 'Oh, *please*, leave him . . .'

But Ken laughed nastily, as he pushed David into the back seat. 'Not likely, you meddling brat.'

Jenny's legs gave way under her and she sat down with a bump on the ground and burst into tears. She heard Dylan rev the engine, and saw a cloud of dirt rise around the back tyres as the car sped away.

A few silent moments passed then Fiona was by Jenny's side. 'Don't cry, Jen! she pleaded, putting her arms around her. 'You were fantastic – so *brave*. You're not hurt are you?'

Jenny shook her head and gave a small smile as Jess began gently to lick her mud-streaked, tear-stained face. 'Poor David,' Jenny said wearily. 'We must get help.'

'Yes,' Fiona agreed. 'Come on, I'll give you a hand up.'

Jenny got shakily to her feet. 'We've got to get back to Windy Hill quickly, Fiona. We'll have to run.'

She patted Jess, then the two girls set off at a sprint towards the track that would lead them home.

8

The girls hardly spoke as they hurried along. The shock of coming across David's makeshift prison, the arrival of the men who held him, and the fight to save Jess, now began to take its toll. Jenny found she was trembling so violently that even her speech came out as a stutter.

'Are you cold?' Fiona asked.

'No! I'm hot.' Jenny shuddered. 'I just can't stop shaking.'

Jess paused once or twice to inspect his sore front

paws, soothing them with a few licks of his tongue. Jenny felt a spasm of guilt as she looked at the torn and bleeding pads. She should never have allowed him to walk so far and work so hard. In spite of it, she was very glad to have had him with her. The men – Dylan and Ken – had seemed genuinely afraid of Jess and he had protected her and Fiona well. She put a loving hand on his smooth head as he trotted along, close beside her.

The sight of the gates to Windy Hill had never seemed so welcoming. Jenny put an arm round Fiona's waist and brought them to a standstill. 'We've made it!' she said, breathless from running. She took a lungful of air and then turned to her friend, 'Fi, listen – I just wanted to say that I'm sorry for getting you mixed up in all of this.'

'*I'm* sorry I wasn't a bit braver,' Fiona replied, biting her lip.

'No, I put us both in danger,' Jenny said, in a small voice, as the truth of what might have happened out in that secluded spot began to dawn on her.

'Well, in the end I think we did the right thing by following Jess.' Fiona smiled weakly, relief in her voice. 'After all, at least we now know what those horrible men look like.'

'And, this time, I've memorised the number plate

of their car,' Jenny said, looking towards Windy Hill.

The high afternoon sun baked down on the red roofs of the farm buildings up ahead. Jenny could see the washing, pegged and fluttering on the line, and the black faces of the sheep as they grazed lazily in the top field. Ellen's carefully tended flowerbeds were a riot of cheerful summer colour. It made a homely and peaceful picture – and it seemed a world away from the desperate scene they had just witnessed.

'Come on, Fi.' Jenny began to run. 'Ellen!' she shouted. 'Dad!'

Ellen appeared on the top step outside the kitchen door, a washing basket under her arm. She shaded her eyes against the sun with a cupped palm. 'What is it, Jenny?' she called pleasantly. But as Jenny drew nearer, her expression changed. She had obviously taken in her stepdaughter's pale face, her shaking hands and her muddy clothes.

Ellen dropped the empty basket on the step and rushed forward to take Jenny in her arms. 'Are you *hurt*?' she asked, looking at Fiona over Jenny's shoulder.

Fiona shook her head slowly and spoke for both of them. 'No, Mrs Miles,' she said. 'We're just scared and tired.'

Jess, came limping up slowly behind the girls, his pink tongue lolling.

'Oh . . . Jess!' Ellen said anxiously. 'What . . .?'

Reluctantly, Jenny pulled away from the comfort of Ellen's arms. 'We have to contact the police,' she said. 'Urgently. And get Dad, too.'

'Oh my *goodness*!' said Ellen. 'What on earth has happened?'

'We found David,' Fiona said, 'but the men came and they've taken him away again. They fought with Jess and Jenny tried . . .'

Ellen held up a hand, her alarm reflected in her eyes. 'On second thoughts, you'd better come inside,' she urged. 'Rest a bit . . . and Jess needs water, by the look of him. It sounds like you'll need to tell the whole story to the police.'

Inspector Moran gratefully accepted the cup of tea Ellen offered him and cleared his throat. 'I must say,' he said, 'you've been very brave, both of you lasses.' He smiled at Jenny and Fiona.

Fraser Miles nodded gravely at his daughter. 'Brave,' he agreed, 'and very foolish.'

'I know,' Jenny said, apologetically. 'We took a chance, Dad.'

'You can say that again,' said her father, grimly.

Jenny felt much calmer, now that she was back at home and they had finished painstakingly describing the events of the afternoon to the police. She and Fiona had had a chance to clean up and Ellen had made them her special hot chocolate to drink. 'Hot, sweet drinks are good for shock,' she had said, as she whipped the milk into a froth.

Jenny was curled up in the big old chair in the sitting-room, looking over Inspector Moran's head at the beautiful picture Carrie's mum had painted of Windy Hill and the surrounding countryside. She had given it to her father and Ellen as a wedding present and it had taken pride of place above the mantel ever since.

'Right,' said the inspector, putting down his cup. 'I won't waste much more of your time. We've got the registration number of the vehicle and, of course, the wallet . . . can you think of anything about either of these men that might, in any way, be unusual? Some, shall we say, distinguishing feature? I know we've been through this before, but now you've had a better look . . .'

'Teeth!' said Fiona, looking at Jenny. 'Remember?'

'Oh, yes,' Jenny made a face as she recalled the unpleasant sight. 'The one called Dylan, the one who drank all that Coke I told you about? Well, he had false teeth. At one point, he took them out!'

The inspector smiled. 'Not a pretty sight, I'll bet!'

'Inspector,' Jenny said, her face suddenly serious. 'Will your officers be able to find this wharf building – the place where they said they were going to take David?'

'My guess is that they were referring to that storage wharf alongside the old whaling station,' Fraser Miles put in.

'Yes. The one just a couple of miles along the coast from Cliffbay,' Inspector Moran said, adding cheerily,

'I've already been on the radio and I feel sure by now my men will have raided the place.'

'Oh *good*!' said Jenny, relieved to think that the police were acting so quickly. Then she sighed. Nobody in the room had put into words what she feared most. Dylan and Ken might have realised that their early conversation about the wharf had been overheard, and decided to take David somewhere altogether different. She dreaded, too, to think what their 'boss' might feel about a meddlesome girl and an aggressive dog that had spoiled their plans so completely.

Inspector Moran stood up and smiled at Ellen. 'A lovely cup of tea,' he said. 'And now, if you don't mind, Mr and Mrs Miles, I'll use your telephone again to speak to the men at the station. Then I'll be off.'

'Of course,' said Ellen, who still looked shaken.

'Oh, and, if you'll take my advice, young lady,' the inspector turned to Jenny, 'it'd be best if you didn't go off anywhere on your own for a few days, just till we round this lot up. OK?' He winked broadly.

'OK,' said Jenny readily. She felt sure that Jess wouldn't want to go out again in a hurry anyway.

'I'll run you home in the truck, Fiona,' Fraser Miles said. 'I'll not have you walking back to Dunraven at dusk, not after a day like today.'

'Thanks,' said Fiona, looking relieved.

While Inspector Moran was making his call, Jenny and Fiona said goodbye.

'You've really been great, Fi,' Jenny said.

'I didn't do enough to help you,' Fiona insisted. 'I was so frightened!'

'But you stuck by me,' Jenny smiled. 'You came along, even when you didn't really think it would be a good idea, and you saw it through.'

'You're so brave, Jenny,' Fiona said, simply. 'I wish I could be like you.' She climbed into the truck beside Mr Miles and waved. 'See you at school tomorrow.'

Jenny waved back. She experienced a warm glow inside. It was a nice feeling to know that Fiona admired her – the way Jenny admired Carrie.

Jenny sat on the kitchen floor between the two dogs, putting an arm round each of them. Orla's tail wagged gently in welcome, but her deep brown eyes lacked their usual glow. Her coat, too, was dull and in need of grooming. Jenny hadn't dared try to brush her, fearing that even the slightest pressure would cause her pain.

She felt again for signs of life, and Orla licked her wrist as she gently probed her tummy. 'I hope, hope,

hope . . .' Jenny whispered. 'Please, Orla, for Carrie. You *must* have a puppy in there. For Carrie.' She dipped her fingers into the bowl of milk and Orla licked them with a warm, dry tongue. *She seems so listless, almost depressed*, Jenny reflected. *She must be missing David.*

Inspecting Jess's feet, she began to feel a bit brighter. The damage was less severe than it had appeared on their return journey from the clearing. Ellen had helped her to bathe his paws while they had waited for Inspector Moran to arrive, and the amount of blood in the bowl had been a shock. Now that they were clean, though, they didn't look nearly as bad.

Jenny kissed Jess's nose. 'You were a star today, my boy,' she said. 'A real hero.'

Ellen came into the kitchen. 'I forgot to tell you, Jenny,' she said. 'Mrs Turner telephoned when you were out today . . .'

'How's Carrie?' Jenny said quickly, her face hopeful.

'Well,' Ellen smiled. 'Carrie has asked her mum to ask you to visit her in hospital – she's feeling much better today.'

'Oh, good!' said Jenny, jumping up. 'That's wonderful news. When can I go?'

'I'm afraid I'm really busy tomorrow,' Ellen said. 'Will the day after be all right?'

'After school? Great!' Jenny was pleased. Then her face suddenly fell. 'She'll want to know all about Orla, and how she's getting on . . . and I'm going to have to *lie* to her. I can't tell her about Orla having been hurt.'

'Best not to,' Ellen agreed. 'Perhaps you could just say that Orla seems fine, and leave it at that.'

'Poor Carrie has been longing to have a dog of her own. I couldn't bear for her to think that Orla might lose her puppies.' Jenny sighed.

Ellen slipped an arm round her and drew her in for a hug. 'I understand how you're feeling, Jenny,' she said softly. Jenny relaxed against Ellen and felt tears prickle behind her eyelids. She blinked them away.

'I'm tired,' she said. 'I think I'd like to go to bed.'

'You do that, love,' Ellen said. 'And try not to think about anything that makes you feel sad. You need a good night's rest.'

Jenny was up in her bedroom, brushing her hair, when she heard a ring on the front doorbell. She glanced at her clock. It was nine o'clock – not the sort of time anyone would pop in for a social visit. It must mean news of one kind or another, she decided. She tightened the cord of her dressing-gown and ran down the stairs in her bare feet.

She recognised the face of the young police officer that had visited Windy Hill previously. 'Hello, Constable Lucas,' she said.

'Have you got some news for us?' Mr Miles prompted, showing PC Lucas into the sitting-room. 'Inspector Moran was here earlier today and he seemed fairly certain that . . .'

'Excellent news,' the young man interrupted, his face beaming. 'Some crack detective work from the young lady here, and her dog, of course, have turned up the result we were hoping for.'

Jenny gasped. 'Really? Have you *found* David?'

'We have indeed – and he's quite safe and well.' PC Tim Lucas bent to stroke Jess, who had wandered away from his basket and come to inspect the visitor.

'Oh! That's *wonderful* news,' Ellen clasped her hands together in relief.

'Yes. Thank heavens for that.' Fraser Miles rubbed his hands through his hair and let out an enormous sigh.

'Fantastic!' Jenny shouted, clapping her hands together and startling Jess. 'And have you arrested the gang?'

'Those of them who had made camp in the old wharf building, yes. The others . . . well, it's just a matter of time. We'll round them up.'

'Where's David now?' Jenny asked eagerly.

'He's at home, with his father. He was very hungry, so I'm told, but otherwise unhurt.' PC Lucas grinned. 'And apparently he's very pleased to have you as a friend, Jenny,' he added.

Jenny laughed. 'I'll bet he's impressed that I turned up *where* I did, *when* I did,' she said.

'Very much so. And, of course, he knows that you gave us the registration number of the vehicle, and the wallet – and an accurate description of his kidnappers, too,' Tim Lucas said.

'Perhaps I should think of joining the force!' Jenny smiled.

'I think the only thing you should be thinking about right now is bed!' said Fraser Miles.

'It's been a long day.' Ellen nodded in agreement.

'OK.' Jenny grinned. A huge wave of relief washed over her. David was safe. He might even be in school tomorrow and he would tell her all about it. 'Goodnight, everyone,' she said, feeling that for the first time in a few nights she really would sleep well.

9

When Jenny woke up on Tuesday morning, her spirits were higher than they had been for a long time. The peculiar churning sensation in her stomach, caused by gnawing worry over David's safety, had left her at last. There was her visit to Carrie in hospital to look forward to, as well. Perhaps she would notice a big change for the better in her friend, Jenny reflected hopefully, as she dressed for school. Carrie might even be out of hospital for the start of the summer holidays, which were not far off.

Brushing her teeth, Jenny drifted off into a pleasant daydream in which she and Carrie were out walking Jess and the new puppy along the cliff path. They were heading for the beach, for a picnic, taking the little collie for his first taste of a splash in the sea.

'How lovely!' Jenny sighed dreamily, twisting her hair into a ponytail. 'How perfect it would be. *Will* be,' she chided herself. '*Will* be.'

Fiona gave a shriek of excitement that attracted more than a few curious stares when Jenny reported in a whisper that David had been rescued by the police.

'Why didn't you *ring* me?' she asked, hopping up and down.

'It was too late,' Jenny said, shifting her heavy schoolbag to the other shoulder. 'I was unbelievably tired, too. But it's great, isn't it?'

'Just imagine!' said Fiona, who seemed struck by the brilliance of their joint detective work. 'If we hadn't followed Jess into the wilderness, and he hadn't found that horrible watery ditch thing that we hid in, we might never have heard the men talking about where they were going to take David . . . and . . .'

'And they might still be searching for him now,' Jenny finished triumphantly. 'Good, isn't it?'

'Brilliant,' she agreed. She looked around. 'Is he

at school, do you know? David?'

'I haven't seen him. Ellen said we should leave him alone for a bit, but I might go round after school today and see him.'

'Does he know about Orla's accident?' Fiona asked with a grimace.

Jenny shook her head. 'Not unless his dad has said anything, but I expect he won't want to worry David with *that* kind of news just yet.'

'Are you going to tell him?' Fiona asked.

'Well, I'll have to really, won't I? But I'm not going to say anything to Carrie. She's got enough problems to cope with at the moment,' Jenny said wisely.

'You're going to . . . lie to Carrie?'

'Yes,' Jenny was determined. 'If I have to, I will. There goes the bell. Fi, do you want to come with me to see David later?'

'I can't.' She wrinkled her nose. 'It's Tuesday. I've got a piano lesson. Yuck.'

'Oh, right . . .' Jenny laughed. 'Well, I'll phone you and tell you how he is, OK?'

Fiona went ahead of her into the classroom. 'OK,' she said. 'Don't worry about how late it is, just ring me. And be sure to tell him I think he's very brave.'

Jenny raised an arm in a cheery wave to her father as

she cycled out of gates to Windy Hill. Below her, to the left, she could see Nell and Jake streaking across the field, weaving expertly in and out of a flock of sheep that had strayed to the furthest boundaries of their land. She could hear the shrill of the whistle that gave the dogs their cue to round up the flock and bring them in for dipping.

Gathering speed, she automatically looked round for Jess, then remembered her pledge to force the collie to rest. He had looked at her pleadingly, pawing at the kitchen door and yapping purposefully, but though she was tempted, Jenny hadn't given in. 'The summer holidays are nearly here,' she told him. 'And then there'll be millions of long walks – but not today. Look after Orla, Jess.'

Now, as she rounded the curve in the unmade road and saw the Fergussons' bungalow ahead, her heart skipped a beat. The police constable had said that David hadn't been hurt during his ordeal, but what if he had been in some way traumatised by his kidnapping and didn't want to see her?

Jenny wished she had had the sense to telephone before leaving Windy Hill. She knocked with a little rat-a-tat-tat, which she hoped sounded friendly, and the door was opened almost immediately by David.

Jenny's fears vanished as she saw him smile.

'Wow! It's you,' he grinned. 'My heroine. Come in.'

'Heroine?' said Jenny, wrinkling her nose. 'I'm no heroine. I almost died of fright. It's Jess you want to thank.' She followed him into the sitting-room.

'Where is he?' David asked eagerly, looking past her, expecting Jess to be following.

'Not here,' Jenny shook her head. 'I didn't bring him. His paws were hurt when he tried to chase the car, and the cuts opened up again yesterday. He's at home, resting.'

'And Orla?' David's eyes were shining. 'Dad told me she was staying at your place, so, thanks for that. How's she getting on?'

'This is nice,' Jenny looked around, changing the subject. The front room was very tiny, but boasted a big bay window which provided a panoramic view of the pale blue sea. 'It's like being in a ship!' Jenny exclaimed. She turned to David. 'How are you?'

'I'm fine – a bit tired. I guess it's from the shock – I thought my last hours had come out there in that smelly old shack. It was horrible.' He flopped onto the sofa, and Jenny sat down opposite him.

'I can imagine,' she said sympathetically.

'I couldn't believe my eyes when Jess, and you, came flying out of the bush . . . it was *great!*' David smiled. 'I owe you one, Jen.' There was a bruise on his temple and a cut on his lip, but other than that he looked the same as he always had.

'Fiona says to tell you that she thinks you were very brave,' Jenny reported.

'Did you tell her everything?' David asked. 'I'm sure everyone at school must be talking about it.'

'No,' Jenny said. 'Nobody knows anything about it. They all thought you were sick – except Fiona, because she was with me.'

'What?' David looked puzzled. 'Really? At the shack?'

'Yep.' Jenny grinned. 'We were out walking Jess when he picked up the scent of the men and became determined that Fiona and I should follow him! So we did.'

'Fiona was hiding, watching everything?'

Jenny nodded. 'I would have stayed hidden, too, if Jess hadn't taken it into his head to try and rescue you by attacking what's-his-name . . . Dylan. And when I saw the knife in that man Ken's hand!' Outrage still surged through Jenny when she pictured Ken's fist gripping the glinting blade, poised above the spine of her beloved dog. 'David,' she said suddenly, 'didn't you *know*? About your father, I mean?'

'I had guessed some of it,' he replied, shrugging. 'It was all a bit weird when we had to leave England in such a hurry to come here. All Dad would say was that I was not allowed to talk about my life in any detail, to anyone. He was so secretive, and . . . nervous, but I understand now that he thought he'd be putting me in danger by telling me what was really going on. To be honest, I was too upset about Mum to care much at the time.'

Jenny nodded, knowing just how that felt.

'And I might have told someone, if I'd known. It's hard *not* to, isn't it?' David asked.

'Yes, hard to keep such a big secret,' Jenny agreed. She paused, then asked, 'What shall I call you now by the way – David or Douglas?'

He shrugged. 'To be honest I'm used to being called David now. Everyone around here knows me as that. I prefer it to Douglas anyway.'

'Oh, good. It would have been difficult to start calling you a different name.' Jenny grinned. 'Will you be moving back to England now that this is all over?'

'I don't think so,' David grinned. 'We like it here – in spite of everything – and my dad has been offered a proper job, too.'

'Oh, that's good. Where?'

'Well, you know he loves wildlife? All animals, actually — that's why he worked for the RSPCA in England. He's going to work as a wildlife conservationist right here on the Scottish Borders.' David looked pleased.

'Remember how we first met?' Jenny mused. 'The day that Jess discovered that oil-covered puffin and your father took us out to rescue the birds on Puffin Island?'

'I can't believe all the things that have happened already since we've known each other.' David laughed.

'There'll be more to come, I'm sure,' said Jenny.

'Starting with the arrival of a litter of Orla and Jess's pups!' David said excitedly.

'Um . . . David,' Jenny began. She coughed and pushed her hair away from her face. 'I haven't got very good news about Orla, I'm afraid.'

David sat up straight, his face suddenly serious. 'What?' he said. 'What do you mean?'

'Didn't you realise that she was struck by the car as it sped away from the green on Sunday?' Jenny said softly.

David stood up, his hands flew to cover his mouth.

'She's fine!' Jenny said quickly, alarmed at how pale he'd gone. 'Honestly, she's doing quite well . . . resting.

It broke two of her ribs, that's all.'

'I heard Jess and Orla barking after they'd pushed me into the back of the car. But my head was in that sack, and Dylan was practically sitting on me . . . I never *felt* anything . . .'

'They hit her sideways, as she tried to cross in front of the car,' Jenny explained. 'It was . . . horrible!'

'Dad didn't say a word! I should have gone to her the moment I was out of there!' David shook his head. 'That's so typical!' He was suddenly angry. 'He never tells me—' He broke off, as the ringing of the telephone cut into his thoughts. He strode away to answer it, asking her as he went, 'But what about the *puppies*, Jenny?'

Jenny didn't get a chance to answer.

'Mrs Miles!' she heard David say. 'Yes, she's here with me. Really? Oh! . . . that's fantastic. She's going to be all right, isn't she? Yes, yes, we'll come over immediately. Thanks. Goodbye.'

'Orla?' Jenny's heart had begun to pound as she sprang to her feet. 'The puppies . . .?'

'Yes! Ellen called Mr Palmer out to Windy Hill. Orla is having her puppies *now*!'

David cycled furiously fast, leaning forward into the wind as though he was trying to win a race, and

Jenny was hard-pressed to keep up with him.

'Slow down!' she pleaded. 'Mr Palmer's there to help her. She'll be fine.'

But David flew on towards Windy Hill, his curly hair pressed against his scalp by his speed, his knuckles white on the handlebars.

Jenny was out of breath when they finally pulled up outside the back door. She hurried to dismount and open the door and David pushed ahead, calling, 'Mrs Miles? We're here – have we missed anything?'

Ellen looked grave as she came to meet them in the porch. 'No,' she said, and gave a big sigh. 'The poor lass is having a wee bit of a battle . . .'

Jenny and Ellen exchanged glances as David stepped into the kitchen. Mr Palmer was kneeling on the floor beside the collie, listening intently, with his stethoscope poised over her heart. Orla raised her head and, at the sight of her master, began to wag her tail weakly.

'Orla!' breathed David and dropped to his haunches. He put out a hand, hesitantly, and smoothed her soft head. The collie looked steadily at David, her sad eyes never leaving his face.

'Mr Palmer . . .?' David whispered.

'David, lad . . .' replied the vet briskly. 'You're not to go getting your hopes up now, do you hear me?

I'm going to do all I can for her, but, if she can't manage it, I'm going to have to take her in to the surgery.'

'But . . . are the puppies all right, Mr Palmer?' Jenny hardly dared to ask the question.

'So far, lass, I think I can feel movement, which is a good sign,' he assured her.

Jenny reached out for Ellen's hand. 'Where's Dad?' she whispered.

'I sent him to find the whelping box he used for Nell. I'm certain he told me it was stored away in one of the sheds.' She squeezed Jenny's fingers and answered the question that she knew would come next. 'I've put Jess in the sitting-room,' she smiled. 'He was behaving very much like an expectant father – pacing around and getting in everyone's way.'

'According to my dates,' Mr Palmer was saying, 'Orla is slightly early having her litter. The normal gestation period is sixty-three days in a dog, but she's only gone sixty; that's fine, but the pups might be a bit on the weak side.'

Jenny watched as Mr Palmer began to clip away the long white hair on Orla's lower body, cleaning and tidying the area to prepare for the arrival of the puppies.

Orla was becoming increasingly nervous. She

tried to get up and yelped in pain as she did so. She flopped back down again and began to pant heavily.

'Oh, poor girl,' murmured David, his eyes like saucers.

'I'll give her something for the pain, now,' Tom Palmer said. 'I would think her whelping is imminent,' he added. 'Her temperature is below 37.8 centigrade.'

'Is that serious?' David asked.

'Normal, laddie,' Mr Palmer assured him. 'Quite normal.'

And suddenly Orla began to strain. As she did so, she whimpered, her head whipping round to lick at her wounded ribs.

'Oh, poor girl,' David said again.

Jenny had her fingers crossed tightly behind her back. *Please*, she begged silently. *Oh, please let the puppies be all right.*

Time passed slowly as Orla heaved and strained, with no result. After fifty minutes, Tom Palmer shook his head. 'I'm not going to let her go any longer than an hour,' he announced. 'If she can't deliver soon, I'll sedate her and take her in.'

Jenny glanced at David. He was biting his lower lip, his eyes fixed helplessly on his dog. Mr Palmer began to prepare to sedate the collie. 'It will have to be a Caesarean operation. It will make things easier for her,' he decided, looking up at David. 'I think the pain is stopping her from contracting successfully and—'

'Mr Palmer! Look!' Jenny shouted. Orla had shuddered and, in that second, a tiny membranous sac slipped away from her body and onto the blanket.

'Aha!' said the vet happily. 'Here we go, then! Good girl. Now, stand back everybody – well back – that's it. Let her have some peace.' Orla began to remove the soft sac with a gentle tongue and then clean her puppy.

Jenny and Ellen, with David between them, huddled on the other side of the room while Mr Palmer stood behind Orla, keeping a close eye on proceedings. The puppies tumbled free of her, trailing their little umbilical cords. Orla sniffed interestedly at each tiny bundle, nosing it over and licking hesitantly. She seemed surprised, and to have temporarily forgotten about the pain in her side.

Jenny clutched David's sleeve during what seemed like an agony of waiting to know whether the puppies were going to be healthy enough to survive. When Mr Palmer had counted four puppies he announced that he suspected that was the lot.

'Are they all alive?' Ellen asked, putting into words

the question that was making Jenny's heart race.

'I'll just check . . .' Mr Palmer examined each pup in turn. They had started to breathe, snuffling and making small mewling sounds that made Jenny want to rush forward and gather them protectively into her arms. But she held back, knowing that it was right that David be the first to enjoy Orla's litter.

'How marvellous! They all seem quite well, if on the small side,' Mr Palmer said. 'This one's a girl,' he said, as he examined the underside of the minute puppy. 'Ah, another girl . . . and yet another girl!'

As relieved as she was that the puppies had been

born alive and unscathed by Orla's accident, Jenny felt a small stab of disappointment. Carrie had so badly wanted a boy puppy.

Mr Palmer picked up the last of the litter and carefully turned it over.

'And the last one is . . . yes, it's a wee boy!'

'Oh, thank goodness!' said Jenny. 'Oh, how lucky! How lovely! I can't believe it.' She threw her arms round Ellen, who hugged her back.

'That's Carrie's pup,' Jenny said. 'That's Charlie – Carrie's gorgeous little Charlie.'

10

Jenny hadn't realised how long she had sat watching Orla with her puppies until Ellen switched on the lights in the kitchen and began to set the table for supper. Reluctantly, she left the four tiny, determined little Border collies that suckled so eagerly from their proud mum, and went to help her.

'They're perfect,' she sighed. 'Aren't they, Ellen?'

'Wonderful,' she smiled. 'Who would have thought Orla could have produced four such healthy pups after the terrible knock she had?'

Jenny looked over at Jess. He lay on his tummy, his tail straight out behind him, looking at the crawling creatures in the whelping box with undisguised fascination. He had been kept apart from Orla, on the orders of Tom Palmer, but had been allowed to view the feeding and cleaning of his offspring from a safe distance.

'You never know,' the vet had warned. 'It sometimes happens that the bitch will attack the male after giving birth. She might see him as a threat to the lives of her puppies.'

Jenny felt she knew differently, but didn't argue. For the time being, Jess seemed content just to look, and every time one of the pups made a tiny squealing sound, his ears pricked up and he cocked his head. Jenny had slipped an old cushion into the wooden box in which Orla lay, and the collie rested against it drowsily, looking up at Jess from time to time.

'Clever boy,' Jenny soothed him. 'You're a dad, now.'

She took the cutlery Ellen handed her. 'I wish . . .' she began, and then felt she was being a bit selfish and stopped.

'What do you wish?' Ellen prompted.

'I know I've got Jess and everything,' she said, 'but I'd *love* to be able to keep a puppy.'

'Here we go again!' Ellen laughed. 'Your dad told

me how determined you were to keep Jess after his birth!'

'But these are Jess's *children*!' Jenny insisted. 'It seems such a shame . . .'

'Well, Mr Fergusson has already found homes for one or two of the females, hasn't he?' Ellen asked, as she put a jug of water of the table. 'And Carrie is going to have the boy.'

'Charlie,' Jenny said, and smiled, adding, 'I suppose you're right.'

'I'm going to ring Mrs Turner to ask her the best time to visit the hospital tomorrow. I'll give her the good news about . . . Charlie, shall I?'

'Oh, yes,' said Jenny happily. 'She'll be so pleased.'

'Supper ready?' asked Fraser Miles, padding into the kitchen in his socks. 'I'm starving.' He glanced over to where Orla lay. 'What a fine whelping box,' he complimented himself.

'It is, Dad,' Jenny smiled. 'Thanks for finding it, and cleaning it out and everything. Orla's very happy in there.'

'Supper won't be long,' Ellen said. 'I've got a phone call to make.'

'How long's she staying? The mother dog, I mean?' Mr Miles asked, opening up the evening newspaper and beginning to browse through it.

'Orla, Dad,' Jenny said. 'Her name's Orla. And she can't be moved until her ribs are mended. As you can see, she's rather busy at the moment!'

Jenny laughed as she saw one of the puppies roll over onto its back, all four, snow-white feet in the air. She loved the milky smell of them, and their screwed up little faces, and the snuffling noises they made.

'Well!' said Ellen, coming back into the kitchen from the hall. 'Carrie's mum has suggested we take Charlie to the hospital for a visit to his owner-to-be!'

'Charlie who?' said Jenny's dad, glancing up.

Jenny gave an exasperated sigh. 'Charlie is the name of the puppy *Carrie's* going to have, Dad,' she said. She turned back to Ellen. 'I think that's a great idea! Could we? Would we be allowed?'

'It seems Mrs Turner has had permission from the oncologist, and Carrie's ward sister, too. A special little room has been set aside for the visit.'

'Oh, wow!' Jenny clapped her hands with excitement.

'It will mean it will have to be a brief visit, Jenny,' Ellen cautioned. 'The puppy won't want to be separated from Orla for very long.'

'OK,' she said.

'David Fergusson gone home yet?' Mr Miles looked idly round the kitchen. 'I thought he was never going to be able to leave.'

'Poor David,' said Jenny. 'He has to go home and I get to spend time with the puppies. It doesn't seem fair.'

'Is he going to be allowed to keep one?' Mr Miles asked.

Jenny shrugged. 'I don't think so.' Suddenly, she looked at her watch. 'Oh, is it too late to phone Fiona? I promised I would – and in all the excitement, I forgot.'

Ellen smiled. 'Go on, then,' she said. 'I'll put the food on the table.'

Imagining Carrie's reaction to her new puppy, Jenny was distracted throughout the school day. She was in a fever of anticipation to get to the hospital and see her friend's face light up in a smile of delight as she cradled Charlie in her arms.

She sat with David and Fiona at break, describing to them every detail of each of the puppies, making Fiona groan with longing. 'I want one!' she cried. 'When can I come and see them?'

'Not today,' Jenny replied. 'I'm taking Charlie to Greybridge Hospital after school.'

For Jenny, the day couldn't end soon enough. She ran up the hill from the bus stop and burst in on Ellen, who was doing the ironing. 'I'm here,' she sang, flinging her schoolbag into a corner. 'I'm ready.'

Ellen chuckled. 'So I see. Right . . . do you want to change?'

'No. Let's just *go*!' Jenny put her arms round Jess and gave him a cuddle, as Ellen found the keys to the pick-up. 'How are your feet?' She peered at the underside of each of the collie's front paws. 'Good. Much better. We'll soon be able to go for a walk.'

'Wrap Charlie in this blanket,' Ellen advised. 'And hold him close to your heart so he can feel it beating. That'll give him comfort.'

Gingerly, Jenny reached out and lifted the tiny puppy. His paws splayed out and he squeaked in protest. Then, feeling the surrounding warmth of the soft blanket, he gave a little sigh and settled back to sleep.

'Orla's just fed them,' Ellen commented. 'So our timing is perfect. He won't be hungry for a while.'

Charlie seemed unconcerned by the jolting of the farm truck. He dozed peacefully in Jenny's arms all the way into Greybridge and she found it almost impossible not to disturb him by kissing his silky head.

★ ★ ★

At the hospital, Jenny and Ellen were greeted by the ward sister, who was expecting them. 'Mrs Turner has just left.' She smiled. 'She usually takes the chance to go home if visitors are coming for Carrie. It gives her a break.' She looked down into the bundle in Jenny's arms. 'Oh! The wee darling! This must be Charlie.'

Walking down the long, sanitary corridors, listening to the tapping of the sister's heels on the linoleum floor, Jenny felt as though she was carrying the most precious gift in the world. Charlie, she felt certain, was going to give her friend a reason to live; the drive to fight the terrible sickness she had battled for so long. The dozing puppy, who had cheated what might have been a cruel fate himself, had no idea how important he was.

'Here we are,' said the sister, dropping her voice to a whisper. 'We're breaking hospital rules letting the dog in here, but we're making an exception in this case.' She winked at Jenny.

The door swung open on a small room furnished like a sitting-room. There was a sofa and two big chairs and television on a table in the corner. Carrie was sitting upright, an expectant smile on her face, her hands clasped excitedly in front of her. 'Oh! Have you brought him, Jen?' she asked.

Jenny went slowly towards Carrie and lowered her arms. 'Here he is,' she said. 'Here's your Charlie.'

Jenny felt she could almost see Carrie's heart turn over as she held the puppy against her chest. Charlie wriggled, and snuffled at Carrie's neck. He laid his warm button nose against her skin and nudged her, then Jenny saw him open his tiny mouth and begin to search for milk.

Carrie laughed, and her face came alive with the

thrill of it. The puppy's pink tongue was warm and as light as a butterfly's wing as he rooted about. Then, finding no sustenance, he gave a small belch and turned round in the blanket to present a full, fat, little tummy for Carrie's inspection.

'He's the most wonderful puppy I've ever seen,' Carrie declared. 'He's just like Jess! Look, four white feet.' She stroked him with a finger.

Jenny took a moment to look at Carrie. They were alone – Ellen and the sister hadn't yet come in. Her friend was wearing a pair of loose pyjamas and a beret that Jenny hadn't seen before. She had lost yet more weight, and the ghostly yellow tinge to her skin was still present. Disappointed, Jenny looked at Carrie's happy face, and she heard her rasping, laboured breath as she gazed adoringly at Charlie.

She began to tell Carrie about the whelping. There were things that had to be left out – Orla's injury, and how she had come to be struck by the car in the first place. Jenny felt this was an especially happy few minutes for Carrie. It would be spoiled by all the horrible details of the last, frightening few days.

'When you're well again,' she said, 'we'll teach Charlie the things that Jess knows. We'll have picnics on the beach in the summer and—'

Carrie was shaking her head, a gentle smile still on

her face. 'I don't know about that,' she said. 'I'm not sure if I'm *going* to come out of here, actually . . .'

Jenny pleaded. 'Don't, Carrie . . .'

'I'm so tired,' Carrie went on, rubbing her finger rhythmically over Charlie's tummy. 'I just want it to be over, Jen, you know?' She held Jenny with clear, steady eyes.

'Over?' Jenny whispered. Her legs felt hollow and her mouth had gone dry.

'Remember the promise?' Carrie wagged a playful finger. 'If I don't make it — and all that — will you keep Charlie for me? You mustn't let him go to anyone else. You must love him as you've loved Jess — and teach him to be as wonderful as Jess is. Will you?'

The blood had begun to drain from Jenny's face and her heart to thud fearfully in her chest. She felt a terrible urge to run from the room, to blot out what Carrie was saying. But she had made a promise. To live life as Carrie would have lived it — gratefully, at a furious pace — and with great courage. She swallowed hard and smiled. 'I remember,' she said solemnly. 'And, of *course* I will!'

Charlie snuggled deeper against Carrie and gave a little sigh of contentment. She lifted him gently and kissed his head. 'Charlie,' she said softly. 'What a beautiful boy you are.' And her face lit up with the happiest smile Jenny had ever seen.

It seemed they had shared only a few minutes when the ward sister's head appeared round the door of the room. 'All right?' she asked, smiling.

'Fine,' Jenny replied steadily.

'I'm afraid you'll have to go now, Jenny lass. I want to get Carrie back to the ward and take her blood pressure.'

'Oh, so soon?'

The sister nodded.

Jenny sat beside Carrie and looked at her, willing her features to mirror the courage she could see in her friend's calm face.

'See you,' she said.

'See you,' Carrie grinned. 'And, Jen? Thanks.'

Wordlessly, Jenny lifted Charlie in his blanket. 'I wish he could stay,' she managed.

'Yes.' Carrie stood up, swayed a little and sat down with a bump.

'Oops! I've got you!' said the sister, grasping her under the arm.

'Bye, Carrie.' Jenny put her arms round Carrie's frail shoulders. Then, quickly, she turned and hurried out of the room.

She fled down the corridor, running from the terrible thought that she might never see her friend again. She found she was searching for Ellen.

'I'm here.' Ellen was beside the hot drinks dispenser. 'I've been waiting.' She put a comforting arm round Jenny, who was very pale. Ellen took the sleeping puppy from her and looked into Jenny's face.

'You didn't let Carrie see you cry, did you?' she asked gently.

'No,' Jenny whispered. 'Why didn't you stay?'

'I wanted you to have time together, just the two of you,' Ellen explained. 'I felt it was important.'

'Is Carrie going to . . .' Jenny couldn't finish the sentence.

'It's not looking too hopeful at the moment, Jenny,' Ellen spoke honestly.

'I saw it in her eyes,' Jenny said simply. 'It was a goodbye – a *for ever* goodbye.'

Jenny climbed the knoll to Darktarn Keep and sat with her back to the ancient wall, looking out over the sea. The stones pressed against her back, imparting the warmth of the sun, sinking now, and leaving a fiery path across the water.

She had walked very slowly, keeping pace with Jess. He stepped lightly. carefully, but was eager to be out and by her side. He seemed to sense her desolation and sat very close, his nose nudging and nuzzling her to offer comfort.

'I can't believe it,' Jenny spoke aloud. 'I can't believe she's not going to get well. It *can't* be true.'

But, in her heart, Jenny knew that it was true. Something she had seen in Carrie's face had convinced her of that. She knew, too, that Carrie was not afraid, and that, in her usual bold-spirited way, she had asked Jenny to visit the hospital in order to say goodbye. Her friend had let go of her struggle.

'And *I've* got to let her go, Jess,' Jenny said softly. 'And be true to the promise. I'm not going to let her down. It's the least I can do.'

For a long time she sat there, listening to the calling of the gulls as they wheeled high above the cliffs. In the quiet, she could hear the waves washing up the beach and the bleating of the sheep across the fields of Windy Hill. The sky turned pink and gold and Jenny, looking up, wondered if there *was* a place up there where people could rest in peace and comfort. It looked so beautiful, she felt sure that there was.

She felt lucky to have had Carrie as a friend. Through her friendship, she had felt herself become strong and whole.

'Come on, Jess,' Jenny stood up. 'Let's go home.'

Picking her way down the side of the hill, she saw

her father and Ellen come out into the yard below. Standing side by side, they watched her.

'Hello, lass,' Fraser Miles said gently, when Jenny reached the bottom.

'Dad?' Jenny looked from one face to the other. Ellen was holding her father's hand so tightly she could see the whites of her knuckles.

'She's gone, Jen,' he said. 'Carrie died an hour ago.'

'Yes,' Jenny nodded. 'I know.' She gave a great, shuddering gasp. 'But she's happier now.'

Ellen looked surprised, but drew Jenny into a hug and began to cry softly.

'I'm thinking about the way she smiled when she held Charlie . . . I'll always remember that smile,' her words were muffled against Ellen's shoulder. 'It was such a *happy* smile!'

'Um, about Charlie . . .' her father began.

Jenny pulled away from Ellen, blinking back her own tears. 'Yes?' she said eagerly.

'Would you like to keep him? Mr Miles asked.

'Oh, yes! I would, Dad,' Jenny smiled. '*Very* much.'

'That's settled then,' he said. 'He'll need training – I'll not have another idle mutt like Jess wasting farm time and . . .'

'Dad!' Jenny was outraged, and then she saw that her father was laughing.

'Only joking, lass,' he said, gathering Jenny up into his arms. She snuggled against the rough wool of his jumper and laid her head there for a second. She thought she was going to cry – cry and cry until her heart snapped in two – but Carrie's smile came up clear and bright in her mind once again.

'Jess! she cried. 'We're going to keep Charlie! Come on, let's go and tell him.'

And she broke free of her father and raced towards the kitchen, her faithful Border collie at her heels.

PIGS AT THE PICNIC
Animal Ark Summer Special

Lucy Daniels

Mandy Hope loves animals more than anything else. She knows quite a lot about them too: both her parents are vets and Mandy helps out in their surgery, Animal Ark.

Mandy and James have won a working holiday at a rare breeds farm. They have a great time helping out with the animals and getting the farm ready to host an important fundraising picnic. Then all the arrangements start to go wrong – especially when the farm pigs get involved! It seems that someone is trying to sabotage the event. But who?

TABBY IN THE TUB
Animal Ark 41

Lucy Daniels

Mandy Hope loves animals more than anything else. She knows quite a lot about them too: both her parents are vets and Mandy helps out in their surgery, Animal Ark.

A feral tabby cat has turned up in Welford and Mandy is worried. The poor thing is about to have kittens and she has no one to look after her. Bill Ward, the postman, comes to the rescue, allowing the tabby to make herself at home in his garden shed. And, before long, the tabby is able to return the favour in a very special way . . .

ORDER FORM

Lucy Daniels

0 340 70438 1	JESS THE BORDER COLLIE 1: *THE ARRIVAL*	£3.99 ❐
0 340 70439 x	JESS THE BORDER COLLIE 2: *THE CHALLENGE*	£3.99 ❐
0 340 70440 3	JESS THE BORDER COLLIE 3: *THE RUNAWAY*	£3.99 ❐
0 340 73595 3	JESS THE BORDER COLLIE 4: *THE BETRAYAL*	£3.99 ❐
0 340 73596 1	JESS THE BORDER COLLIE 5: *THE SACRIFICE*	£3.99 ❐
0 340 73597 x	JESS THE BORDER COLLIE 6: *THE HOMECOMING*	£3.99 ❐
0 340 77847 4	JESS THE BORDER COLLIE 7: *THE DISCOVERY*	£3.99 ❐
0 340 77849 0	JESS THE BORDER COLLIE 9: *THE PROMISE*	£3.99 ❐
0 340 73599 6	PIGS AT THE PICNIC	£3.99 ❐
0 340 73598 8	TABBY IN THE TUB	£3.99 ❐

All Hodder Children's books are available at your local bookshop, or can be ordered direct from the publisher. Just tick the titles you would like and complete the details below. Prices and availability are subject to change without prior notice.

Please enclose a cheque or postal order made payable to *Bookpoint Ltd*, and send to: Hodder Children's Books, 39 Milton Park, Abingdon, OXON OX14 4TD, UK.
Email Address: orders@bookpoint.co.uk

If you would prefer to pay by credit card, our call centre team would be delighted to take your order by telephone. Our direct line *01235 400414* (lines open 9.00 am–6.00 pm Monday to Saturday, 24 hour message answering service). Alternatively you can send a fax on *01235 400454*.

TITLE		FIRST NAME		SURNAME	

ADDRESS
DAYTIME TEL: POST CODE

If you would prefer to pay by credit card, please complete:
Please debit my Visa/Access/Diner's Card/American Express (delete as applicable) card no:

Signature .... Expiry Date: ....

If you would NOT like to receive further information on our products please tick the box. ❐